EVA AND THE WINTER OF 63

Eva and the Winter of 63

Malcolm J. Brooks

authorHOUSE®

AuthorHouse™ UK Ltd.
1663 Liberty Drive
Bloomington, IN 47403 USA
www.authorhouse.co.uk
Phone: 0800.197.4150

© 2014 Malcolm J. Brooks. All rights reserved.

No part of this book may be reproduced, stored in a retrieval system, or transmitted by any means without the written permission of the author.

Published by AuthorHouse 05/13/2014

ISBN: 978-1-4969-7996-4 (sc)
ISBN: 978-1-4969-7997-1 (e)

Any people depicted in stock imagery provided by Thinkstock are models, and such images are being used for illustrative purposes only. Certain stock imagery © Thinkstock.

This book is printed on acid-free paper.

Because of the dynamic nature of the Internet, any web addresses or links contained in this book may have changed since publication and may no longer be valid. The views expressed in this work are solely those of the author and do not necessarily reflect the views of the publisher, and the publisher hereby disclaims any responsibility for them.

Dedication

This book is dedicated to the three Ms, my Musketeers, Margaret, Melanie and Martin; friends for life and beyond and to the Rocky Mountaineer where the whole adventure began.

Thanks

Once again my very great thanks go to Barbara, Carol, Margaret A, Margaret B and Andrew for all their hard work and support. Your work here is now at an end. It's time for the wonderful and very special Eva to move on!

Guns and sledges

The droplets of blood fell onto the frozen snow. They fell at regular intervals and as they hit the hard frozen surface they threw out a red ring of smaller droplets, much like the effect of a firework in the sky.

I wiped my hand across my face. Yes, it was my blood dripping as regularly as the beats of a metronome.

How I got in this position, on all fours staring at the ever-increasing pool of blood, was a mystery to me.

The last recollection I had was of being behind the trenches somewhere in France (or was it Belgium?) and sometime in 1916? The night sky had been alive with the sound of guns. There had been smoke and fire everywhere.

My thoughts were interrupted by the sudden appearance of two boys, both probably in their early teens.

"We are ever so sorry missus," said the slightly older looking one.
"You suddenly just appeared from nowhere and we couldn't get out of your way!" said the other.

It was then that I noticed that my left ankle was throbbing. I tried to stand but it was too painful. Being on all fours was the best position for me, despite the continual loss of blood from my nose.

The younger boy offered me a handkerchief to stem the flow of blood. I hesitated for a moment and then graciously accepted the offer, germs and all.
"Where am I?" I asked.
The boys looked at each other.
"Ferry Fryston," came the simultaneous reply.

Vaguely, I remembered that once, a long time ago, I had lived in Ferry Fryston.
"This might seem a stupid question, but what year is it?"
Again they looked at each other as if to say 'has this lady escaped from some form of mental institution?'

"It's New Year's Day of 1963," the younger one said, as if to give me the benefit of the doubt that the year had only just changed.
"1963," I repeated thoughtfully.
"I'll go and get my father," said the older-looking one, "You don't look as if you can walk very far. I only live on Elmete Drive which isn't far. Just a minute," and off he ran, leaving me and the younger boy to make polite conversation.

"What's your name?" I asked.
"Alan."
"And your friend?"
"He's called Derek."
"Do you live close by?"
"Yes, on St Andrew's Road, just down there."

That name rang a bell. I used to live at number 17 St Andrew's Road. I couldn't really tell him that as he might ask me a question and I hadn't been born yet!
"I think that this is the bag you were carrying when we hit you."
He picked it up and placed it a little closer to where I was now sitting. As he did so, the bag toppled sideways and a gun fell out.

Alan looked shocked that, in his terms, an old lady wandering around on a dark early evening should possess a gun. In truth I was nearly fifty-four years old and had he looked in the bag he would have seen five more. All were First World War pistols.

It didn't take long for Derek to return with his father who introduced himself as Michael O'Rourke.
"I'm Eva," I said apologetically, "I am sorry to have caused you so much trouble."
"I have told Derek a hundred times that using this hill as a sledge run was dangerous. These pathways have been covered in snow and ice for weeks."

Derek looked dutifully admonished but repeated "she just appeared from nowhere," which although it would seem unlikely to his father, was probably the truth.

Alan tried to help his friend.
"She wasn't there when we started at the top of the hill, we checked, then suddenly, half-way down, bang we hit her!"

Michael looked disbelievingly at the two boys.
To be fair to them they were having fun in the snow and I spoiled it. However this wasn't the time to explain how I had suddenly appeared from nowhere, but Alan wasn't finished defending his friend.

"She's got a gun!" He bent down and picked up the one that had fallen out of my bag and was half-hidden in the snow.

Michael and Derek looked a bit taken aback by Alan's revelation. The same question must have been in their minds. What was a lady of my age doing walking the streets in the early evening with a gun?
I tried to explain. "I own an antique shop in the town and the guns in that bag are just replicas. I have bought them from a friend in St Andrew's Road. I was on my way to get the bus back to town when the accident happened."

It was the best I could do. The first part was correct. I did own an antique shop in the town but it wasn't going to be there for another fifty years. The rest of what I said was downright lies. The guns were real pistols from the First World War. I know that because I had just 'bought' them from a soldier who was looking after the stores just behind the front lines, moments before 'all hell let loose'!

Eva and the Winter of 63

There is a time for telling the truth and a time for telling lies and in this case, the latter was the only sensible option.
"Let's get you into the warm and see what damage the boys have done to your ankle and face."

With the help of Michael and Derek, I hobbled the hundred or so metres to their house. It was a typical semi-detached council house that had been built in the 1950s. I know because I had spent my entire childhood living in such a house.

Since the 'cat was out of the bag' so to speak, I let Alan carry the bag that contained the six pistols which were destined to be sold at Eva's Antique Emporium on Carlton Street in the year 2048.

Michael's wife Sheila was a nurse and her assessment was that I had broken my left ankle, presumably when the front edge of the sledge that Alan and Derek were riding on had hit me. The injury to my nose might have been as a result of the bag of guns hitting me in the face.

Michael arrived with a cup of tea, the universal panacea for all ailments. It was clear that Michael and Sheila had been discussing what best to do with me.
"We ought to take you to Hightown Hospital and get that ankle X-rayed," said Sheila "with all that swelling I am certain that it is broken."

I had no idea what Hightown Hospital Accident and Emergency department was like in the 1960s, but if it was anything like the time when I was in my teens in 2010 it would mean a long, long wait.

"I think I will be OK. I'll have a rest and then go and catch the bus home. The ankle will probably be alright by tomorrow."

Michael and Sheila looked at each other and it was a look of concern. Whether it was a look of concern for me I wasn't sure and then Michael said, "I spent some time in the army and those guns are real and not replicas. Who was the friend you bought them from?"

I paused for thought. Quite often following one lie with another only gets you into further trouble. "I can't say. It would get my friend into trouble."

Michael left the room, to do what I can only guess. I picked up the cup of tea that had been placed before me on the table.

"That's an unusual watch," said Derek, "it has no clock face on it, only numbers. Can I look at it?"

As if matters couldn't get any worse, my digital watch had been invented well after 1963. I took it off slowly and handed it to him. My heart was doing somersaults. Could I risk telling them the truth?

Suspicious minds

Whilst Derek was examining my digital watch and I was trying to think of yet another lie, there was a knock at the door. Shortly after, Michael entered the living room with another teenage boy.

"Look at this watch John. It's fab!"
The teenager took the watch and examined it.
"It works with only numbers and it's from Japan." I lied.
"You've been to Japan?"
"Yes, as part of my job collecting antiques," yet another lie.

"It's called a digital watch as opposed to the analogue watch you all have. It's more accurate so they say. They are trying to develop these in Japan and this was given to me as a present." This lying was getting far too easy.

The boys seemed impressed, even if Michael was not. He had already spotted one of my lies so didn't seem too willing to take what I said at face value.

At that moment, I looked at John and had a vague feeling I had seen those eyes before. His demeanour too seemed familiar.

"I thought that we were going sledging again tonight?" John said to Derek as he handed back my watch.

"We've already been," replied Alan "but sadly we had an accident and knocked this lady over. Mrs O'Rourke thinks that she has broken her ankle."

"I'll be alright," I repeated, "it's only bruised. I'll be as right as rain tomorrow."

Another knock at the door sounded, but this time much louder. Michael left the room to answer it.

"I'd have taken more care," John said as if to add to his friends' discomfort.

"She just appeared from nowhere," repeated Alan in their defence.

The living room door opened yet again and Michael reappeared, this time with a policeman.

"I'm sorry about this Eva but I had to inform PC Evans about the guns. There has been a lot of news lately about Russian spies. The John Profumo scandal has made everybody very aware of what might be going on."

I hadn't a clue who this John Profumo was but being linked to spying for the Russians seemed a bit far fetched.

"You think that I am a Russian spy?" I exclaimed.

"There are a few things that don't add up. You lied about the guns being real and where you got them from, and then that watch is not Japanese. I suspect that it's Russian technology."

"I don't think that this lady quite fits the Christine Keeler and Mandy Rice-Davies image, do you Mr O'Rourke?" Everyone turned to look at John; they seemed surprised at him knowing about these two ladies.
"Anyway," Michael continued, "PC Evans would like to ask you a few questions, if that's OK with you Eva?"
"Fine, ask away," I said resignedly.
"Can we do this in private?" PC Evans asked Michael.
"Of course, you can use the kitchen."

Mrs O'Rourke had found me a walking stick which apparently belonged to her late mother. I rose from the chair and hobbled off after PC Evans. We went out of the living room, through the hallway and into the kitchen. This house was exactly the same design as the one in which I had spent all my childhood days and which was situated just around the corner.

"I'm ever so sorry about this but as Mr O'Rourke has said there are a lot of people in high places who are worried about the recent scandals."

I felt that it would not be appropriate to ask him what these scandals were about as that would only make matters worse. I suspected that the two ladies that John had mentioned were possibly spies who had used their womanly charms to gain state secrets.

"I know that it doesn't seem right that I have six guns in my possession but you must believe me when I

say that I collect antiques. These guns are clearly old ones from the First World War and not new Russian technology as Mr O'Rourke thinks."
"Yes, Mr O'Rourke showed me one of them and they are definitely not Russian or new, but why won't you tell us where you got them from?"

"It's difficult and you wouldn't believe me if I told you the truth."
"Try me Mrs . . . ?"
"Just call me Eva."
"OK Eva, where did you get them from?"
"I got them from the First World War."
"That's impossible! You're too young."
"No I'm not. I am nearly sixty and was born in 1903 and was fifteen when the war ended," I lied yet again. "Many of my relations kept their guns after the war and I know I shouldn't have but I collected them as souvenirs. It is only now that I dare put them up for sale in my shop."

He looked unconvinced. "Where exactly is your shop Eva?"
"Carlton Street," I said as confidently as I could. I was hoping that by the time he could check this information I would be out of Ferry Fryston and out of 1963.

Reflections

To most people travelling through time must seem like an exciting power they would love to possess. In truth it has been a mixed blessing. I have seen and been in the midst of some horrific scenes and yet it has been my life for fifty-three years.

My first recollection of seeing what most people call 'ghosts' happened in my bedroom in the year 2000 when I was five years old. As coincidence would have it the 'ghost' that I first met had the same name as me, Eva.

I was never really frightened of her because she was so sweet, you know, the kind of sweet that comes with grandmothers. Sadly, she had died in my bedroom on 25th May 1963.

I had some difficulty making people believe that I could see Eva and my sisters, Sharon and Sophie, both thought I was slightly mad or a bit of a drama queen. It wasn't until I was about 11 years old when I was playing rugby in next door's backyard that I met John. David, the boy next door, kicked the ball a little too hard and it went over the fence and John caught it.

I didn't know why he was standing there but I had noticed him before from the window of our house. I had seen him walk past my house on a couple of occasions and had assumed he too lived on St Andrew's Road.

It transpired that he used to live in my house when he was young and was going through the reminiscing stage of his life, much in the same way as I am doing now.

We became friends because he was the only one at that time who believed I could see people who had died. In fact, the sweet old lady that I could see in my bedroom, it turned out was his Nanna Eva.

My 'special powers', as John called them, allowed me to go back in time through what Nanna Eva had called 'corridors of transit'. By walking through any ghost that would let me and down a bright corridor of light, I could enter the world at the time of their birth or death.

It may sound a bit selfish but I did use my 'special powers' to start up my business in the antique trade. An unfair advantage, you might say, as I could retrieve my antiques by choosing the right ghost, so to speak.

Along with Nanna Eva, I had a number of other 'friends' from the spirit world and they allowed me to visit any century as far back as the 16th century. I never fancied going any further back even if I could. The 16th and 17th centuries were bad enough but at least they provided me with the genuine articles I could sell in the 21st century.

Yes, I know, it was theft on a large scale, but it was undetectable, easyish and lucrative at a time when jobs were difficult to come by and I was using my talents as my teachers had encouraged me to do!

By the time I was thirteen I had visited the 17th century twice. These two adventures had brought me into contact with Valentine who had died in 1644 at the Battle of Marston Moor near York during the English Civil War.

It was through wanting to help him out that I learned just what my special powers allowed me to do. Seeing both the living and dead and sometimes not being able to distinguish between the two has brought me some very awkward moments. The clue was usually how they were dressed but with the many weird and wonderful fashions of today in 2048 it was not always easy.

Quite rightly, when John died, he left all his money to his wife Ann and his two children Paul and Jayne, but John had written into the joint will that I could buy their special bungalow for a reasonable sum of money when Ann died.

I say 'special bungalow' because prior to it being built, the land it sat on had been occupied by a church. Well,

I say a church, but it was really a sort of corrugated structure that had been used as a church and had been called St James' Mission Church. It was connected to a 'proper' church some two miles away and had the same Rector to administer services.

The bungalow was where, from time to time, I met John and Valentine. I had married David, the 'boy next door', the very person who had inadvertently introduced me to John and we had had three children, Charlotte, Jacob and Rosalind.

As far as I knew, none of them had my special powers and I was determined to keep from them the murky world that their mother inhabited from time to time.

At times, this was difficult, as I would suddenly arrive in the bungalow, back from an antique collecting session, to be met with 'where did you spring from, we didn't know that you were home'. I had become somewhat adept at lying and giving false excuses. I wasn't proud of myself for developing this characteristic but it was necessary if I was going to keep my life-style a secret.

My husband David, fortunately or unfortunately, spent a lot of time away from the family home, but even then there were times when I sprang from nowhere to give him quite a shock.

He spent a lot of time in China which had had a great influence in the UK over the last twenty years. He was working on a collaboration project with them to develop the latest in 'immersive technology' in which

Eva and the Winter of 63

our digital and physical worlds seamlessly intertwined; a way in which our biology and the technology merged. He often talked about nano-sized technology that could be worn behind the ear or on the hand, invisible to the naked eye but capable of sensing things and having the potential to make us live longer.

Special glasses had been developed a number of years ago which contained a micro-sensor able to detect the person's face the user was looking at. Linked to a database, the wearer was able to identify and name people as they met them. Other information about the person such as birthday, age, family they had and occupation could also be flashed onto the screen within the glasses. The current collaboration project that David said he was working on had the onerous task of trying to retrieve only that information the wearer wanted and this was to be controlled by their thought processes, together with reduction in size of the technology that could make this happen. His research, he said, had also helped in the development of artificial limbs being controlled by thought and the wider use of 'graphene', a light but extremely strong and flexible alloy.

The whole family nicknamed me the 'magician' because of their perception that I disappeared and reappeared so quickly. To tell them the truth would have meant that I would have had to embroil them in my life-style just as I had done with John and this would not have been fair on them. I could cope with the nickname and play up the fact that I could appear from nowhere.

David did, I think, have his suspicions, but they were more 21st century ideas that I was a drug dealer of some sort!

My present predicament was as a consequence of a visit to 1916 to 'find' guns from that period for customers who had asked me to get them. I remembered being with a regiment of Yorkshire soldiers, well behind the battle lines and doing a bit of business with a Quartermaster to obtain the six guns that Alan had accidently found in the bag I was carrying when they hit me.

The Quartermaster was in charge of the stores which contained various items that the soldiers needed, including guns. What we were doing was completely illegal and very dangerous. I was in fact bribing him with cigarettes, which at that time were a very good currency. I had had to get the cigarettes from the 1960s because cigarettes from the 21st century all carried severe health warnings as to their dangers and these might not have gone down too well in the trenches of 1916. The irony was that being in those trenches was far more dangerous than smoking a packet of Woodbines. 'These cigarettes can kill', whereas being in thick mud in those trenches with bullets and shells all around . . . ?

What had happened next was not clear even now. I had 'bought' the guns and was leaving with them in a bag when shells started to explode all around. The Germans must have broken through the British lines and were bombarding the stores and temporary hospital areas.

I must have panicked and ran into the hospital. The next thing I knew was that Alan's and Derek's sledge hit me and I was dripping blood. The only thing that I could think of was that I had inadvertently run through a ghost and down his or her corridor of transit to the place where the sledge hit me. Why that should be the place where the corridor took me was a complete mystery to me.

The not so great escape

PC Evans left the kitchen, presumably to talk to Michael about what to do with me. He hadn't asked me the obvious question about where I lived, unless he assumed I lived over the top of my shop in Carlton Street. The bungalow I actually did live in hadn't been built yet and was still a mission church.

Plans for an escape were formulating in my brain but with hardly being able to walk I couldn't really make a run for it.
I needed a ghost. Why was there never one around when I needed one?

At that moment the three boys, Derek, Alan and John, came into the kitchen.
"Have you three been sent to make sure I don't do a runner?" I joked.
Derek spoke. "No, of course not, but we have been talking and feel ever so guilty about getting you into

trouble with the police. My father shouldn't have involved them."

"Look," I said, "I cannot tell you the truth, although one day I promise I will. I am not a burglar or a Russian spy but perhaps what I have done is not quite right. Can you help me to escape from PC Evans, just while I get matters sorted out? It shouldn't take long." I felt really bad involving the boys in some form of escape but it was the only thing that I could think of at that moment.

"They won't take you to prison with a broken ankle. They'll probably just take you to hospital to get it fixed," said John sympathetically.
"Yes, but they will keep a guard on her so she doesn't escape," warned Alan.
"She couldn't do a runner even if she tried!" said John with that big grin on his face which yet again was so familiar to me.
"We could use your sledge John to move Mrs . . . ?"
"Eva, just call me Eva," I replied to Derek's suggestion.
"We could use your sledge to move Eva away from PC Evan's clutches," he repeated.

"It would be easy to follow the tracks of a sledge through the snow."
"I could use my sledge with a weight on to set up different tracks," said Alan.
"OK, that's a good idea. Where are we going to hide her?" asked Derek.
"We have a large garden shed that my Dad uses which, since we have all this snow and ice, he never goes in," replied John.

"OK, that's the plan, but we will have to be quick about it. PC Evans will be back soon," said Derek, "I'll go and see if I can keep the adults occupied for a time longer whilst you slip out of the back door with Eva."

"Alright Eva come on, hold on to Alan and me. The sledge is at the side of the house."
"I hope that you boys are not going to get yourselves into a lot of trouble in aiding a suspected criminal to escape?"
"It's the best bit of excitement we've had around here since the police came to arrest old Mr Afford for fiddling his electricity meter!"

Derek left to do his best to keep the three adults in the living room for as long as possible.

It was really dark at the back of the house but what little light there was gave the snow an eerie glow. With a gentleness that belied their years, Alan and John placed me on the sledge. Although the years had slightly expanded my waistline, I was only about nine and a half stone so the boys had little trouble pulling the sledge; it was just a question of balance!

Alan went off to do his decoy runs leaving John to pull the sledge on his own. Fortunately, John said that it wasn't too far to his house. As the journey progressed memories of forty years ago came flooding back. This was the street where I had spent my childhood, playing jacks, whip and top and doing my favourite pastime of skipping, together with the 'hide and seek' and 'tig' games that had expended so much of my energy.

A kind of foreboding swept through my body as we passed The Green, scene of so many ball games, and on up the slight incline.

"What number do you live at, John?" I asked.
"Number 17," he puffed.
It hit me like a thunderbolt. That smile, the sense of humour and now the house number 17 on St Andrew's Road.

This was most certainly the young John who later in his life was to accompany me twice to the 17th century. My stomach was doing somersaults. I was so pleased that I had not succumbed to telling the boys about my time travelling abilities. If I had I might have changed the course of history. Had John known about a lady called Eva who could travel through time it would have altered the whole course of our first meeting or was it our second. This was getting all too complicated for me to understand.

John opened the gate that I had opened so many times before and pulled the sledge up the path that I had walked, run and skipped along but this was the first time that I could remember going up it on a sledge.

Clearly John's parents did not own a car, as the one obvious difference between 1963 and the 21st century was that there was no garage present. Instead there stood a large garden shed. John opened its door. There was no lock on the shed which was a sign of the times. During my childhood sheds and garages needed locks, if for no other reason than for insurance purposes.

Without locks the insurance was invalid if anything was stolen. Things would have certainly been stolen in my childhood days if no sturdy lock was in place.

The inside of the shed was full of tools for various household and garden jobs.
"We need to get you some blankets to make you more warm and comfortable. Maybe we need to get you another coat, a hat and some gloves," John was being very practical and thoughtful.

I had not really dressed for snow and ice. The inside of the windows of the shed were thick with ice, a sign of how cold it was, and indeed how much colder it was going to become.

At least with the rest and cold, my ankle should get some of the necessary requirements to repair itself, provided no serious bones had been broken. If I could elevate the ankle slightly and maybe get a bandage to compress it, the repair might take less time and then I could get back home sooner rather than later.

"If you could find a bandage John, it would help."
"I'll see what I can do."

The shed, despite its contents, had quite a space in which I could rest. After John had left, I tried to make myself comfortable in a fold-up chair that John had set up and, on my insistence, a second chair on which I could put my foot. I settled down to wait for John's return.

Eva and the Winter of 63

The cold was really getting to me and I rubbed my hands for warmth. It was about twenty minutes before John returned with a blanket and a pillow, gloves and a scarf.

"I'm sorry it took so long, but Mum was a bit reluctant to let me go out again. Dad is on 'afternoons' and doesn't get back until about 11 o'clock. She likes me to be with her during the evenings when Dad is at work as she has Nanna and Grandad staying with us at the moment because Nanna isn't too well."

All this I knew. In fact I knew that Nanna Eva would die of cancer on the 25th May, as little as five months away but this was one piece of information I was definitely going to keep to myself. One of the many downsides to my time travel was that occasionally I knew what was about to happen. I had used this to my advantage on a number of occasions but this was one of those sad pieces of futuristic knowledge you had to live with.

"I've been thinking," I said to John, "maybe it's a little too obvious that at the time I go missing from the O'Rourke's house, so do you and Alan. Won't this be one of the first places that they will look for me?"

"I hope Alan has done a good job with the tracks and the weather is just too bad for them to search. The snow has begun to fall again. It looks like another blizzard is on its way. We can only wait and see what tomorrow brings and maybe we can find you somewhere else to hide in the morning. The O'Rourkes might just think that since it was getting late, Alan and

I had to go home. Both our mothers are quite strict on the times that we must be in by."

"How quaint," I thought. Not something that happened when we were young. 'I'll be in about ten, Mum' could mean anything around midnight although Dad was never too pleased if he had returned from the pub before we got in.

"Do you need any food or drink?"
"No thank you."
He turned to leave again. "Goodnight. I'll fetch you something to eat and drink tomorrow morning. We're still off school, so I'll be able to come and see you at regular intervals."

"John," I said slowly, "you do believe that I'm not a Russian spy don't you?"
"Why, of course I do. According to the films, all the female Russian spies are young and beautiful." And with that he departed.

I had been young and sort of beautiful once upon a time and when he meets me again in 2006 I will make a point of telling him, if, of course, I can remember!

I settled down for what I believed would be one the coldest nights of my life. It was well below freezing and likely to get colder as the night progressed. At least the blanket was thick and the pillow soft.

I started to think about my predicament and what I could do to get out of it without the possibility of going to prison in the year 1963. I had seen some old TV programmes about what the police were like in the 1960s and 70s and their methods of 'obtaining' information, and to be fair the prospect of being interrogated did not fill me with any joy at all.

Strangely, whilst I wished to get home to the safety of 2048 as soon as possible, a small part of me wanted to stay and help John through a very difficult time with the forthcoming death of his beloved Nanna Eva. Although he didn't know it now, we were going to go through really difficult times together in the 17th century; two adventures that would live with him until his dying day. The irony of the situation was that I had been a teenager at the time of our adventures and he had been nearly 60 years old, so the roles in my current situation were nearly reversed. I had been a precocious teenager and had caused him a lot of heartache and trouble, but now here he was again being so helpful to me, someone he knew so little about. I really should be less selfish and pay back some of the kindness he had shown me.

Tea and toast

Even though I drifted off to sleep from time to time, as I expected it was the worst night that I had ever experienced. I felt chilled to the bone. Surely it could not have been any colder outside the shed than in it!

By the time John arrived in the morning I felt really bad. I was shivering uncontrollably and my ankle felt like a block of ice.
John just took one look at me and said, "I'll go fetch my mother," and before I had chance to stop him he was gone.

After a further few minutes of shivering, he returned with a petite woman of about forty years of age. She wore quite thick glasses but had a smile that was so reassuring. There was no sense of accusation or recrimination, just concern on her face for my situation.

Eva and the Winter of 63

"Hello, I'm Pearl, John's mother. We really do need to get you to the hospital. You look very ill."
I smiled weakly, knowing that she was right in her assessment of the situation.

She addressed her son. "John, go down to the O'Rourke's house and ask Sheila if we can use their phone to phone for an ambulance."

I assumed that not many people on the estate had phones in their homes and perhaps being more professional the O'Rourke's were the exception. Stupidly, I almost offered Pearl my mobile phone which was in my pocket. Somehow, through the numbness, my brain just stopped my mouth from making this ridiculous suggestion.

Before John had time to leave, his mother added, "If no one is in at the O'Rourke's house then you will have to go up to the phone box at the New Shops and dial 999."

Some things never change and although in the 21st century there had been a number of attempts to change the emergency services number to 911 and 123, it had remained the same. The argument against 999 had always been that with mobile phones accidently holding the nine key down and accidently pressing 999 was more of a possibility than 911 or other numbers. Inevitably there had been many false 999 calls, but the number was deep-seated in British culture and the change never happened.

"John tells me that you were knocked down by Alan and Derek. They can be reckless at times, after all they are teenage boys and a little bit of danger is what they enjoy. They haven't been through a war and hopefully they never will. When my husband Harry was eighteen, just five years older than John, he was enlisted to fight in the Second World War."

I had read about the boys who had been born in the late forties and fifties. Something about the fact that they had never had a war to fight and so turned into punks, anarchists and football hooligans as a substitute.

"I'll go and make you a nice hot cup of tea. Do you think I can help you into the house where it's definitely warmer than this shed? Do you think you could manage it? I should have thought about that before I sent John off."

I struggled to my good foot and slowly hopped, holding on to anything I could including Pearl. Eventually, in time, and in a lot of pain I made it into that familiar kitchen. There were a number of small differences, the biggest of these being that there was a hatch which linked the kitchen with what I know to be the living room or as we called it, the lounge. There was no central heating and although it was a bit warmer, it did not have the double glazing and under-floor heating that I had grown up with. In fact, it was still pretty cold and the windows had ice on the inside just as the shed had.

"Let's go through into the living room. It's warmer in there as I've just lit the fire."

I staggered the few metres into the living room and then another five metres to where the fire was struggling to create some heat.
There was an old iron mesh thing that I had never seen before and lots of paper in the hearth. I wasn't too familiar with fires in houses although I did have a faint recollection of having seen them in some old houses.

"I need to mend the fire," Pearl said and then proceeded to do one of the strangest things I have ever seen done in a living room! She took some of the paper from the hearth and opened it out. She pushed the iron mesh thing against the wall over the fire and put the paper partially over it. The air seemed to suck the paper so it stuck to it. I could only assume that this bizarre process allowed air to be drawn under the paper and into the burgeoning fire.

"I'll go get that cup of tea," Pearl said as she left the room. What happened next was, for me, quite frightening.

I noticed that, through the paper, the flames seemed to be flickering a little more with the sudden rush of air. The centre of the paper started to turn brown and then suddenly burst into flames!

"Pearl!" I screamed, "it's on fire!"
She rushed in and then stopped and smiled.

"It's OK love. That sometimes happens. I'll put some more paper on the fireguard and draw it again," and nonchalantly she removed the paper that had burnt itself out, opened up more paper and put it on the 'fireguard'. "The fire will be OK soon. It does take some doing on these cold mornings. When it has caught hold a bit more I'll put some more logs and coal on and then we can do some toast. You won't have eaten yet, will you?"

"No," I said, not quite having recovered from the burning paper.
"Harry'll be up in a moment. He is on 'afternoon' shifts this week, so doesn't get in until late and therefore he likes to lay in a bit. He doesn't start work 'til two. It's better than him doing 'nights', we all have to be very quiet then!" She laughed and went to fetch the tea.

When she arrived back in the living room she was carrying a tray containing two cups and saucers, a teapot, a milk jug, a sugar bowl and a strange looking long three pronged fork-thing and a plate of sliced bread. I say sliced bread but it wasn't the sort of sliced bread you could buy when I was young. This bread had been cut by hand and was really thick.

"I thought we would be posh," she said, "with a milk jug and not the bottle! Do you like your milk in first? It is always best you know. I'll just wait for the tea to mash a bit longer."

I had to smile. Not only did I not get to answer the 'milk in first' question but the term mash had a different meaning to me. My mother always made tea for two

Eva and the Winter of 63

straight into the mugs with the tea bag, a tea pot was reserved for family gatherings.

"Oh, just a minute, I've forgotten something," and off she trotted to the kitchen.
I was definitely feeling a little better and warmer. I studied the pronged thing that was on the tray. I had no idea what it could be used for in the tea-making ceremony that was about to happen.

The paper burst into flames again but this time I didn't panic.
"That fire looks better now. I'll add some more sticks of wood and a bit of coal. Harry gets it free on account of his work," Pearl said as she returned with yet another strange looking object that resembled a small sieve.

I watched her as she set about the tasks that I suppose she did every day of her life. She poured the milk into the two cups. I hadn't the heart to tell her that I liked my tea black!

Then she took the 'sieve' and placed it on the first cup and poured the tea through it. Of course, it was a sieve for catching the tea leaves. No teabags for Pearl; a woman of tradition. She repeated the same process with the second cup.

"Do you take sugar?"
"I'd prefer a sweetener if you have one, thanks."
She gave me a puzzled look. "A what love?"
"Do you have any sweeteners, like Canderel or Sweetex?"
"Sorry love, I don't know what you mean."

"Oh, it's OK, I'll have sugar then."
She hesitated as if still thinking about my request.

She added the sugar and stirred both cups, before handing mine to me. "How many slices of toast do you want?"
"Oh, just the one please."
"OK." She proceeded to carry out yet another strange task. She took the top really thick slice of bread and stuck the three-pronged thing into it, lifting it up as she did. She lent over the improving fire and put the bread as close to the flames as she dare without burning it.

"It's always easier if you have a fire with no flames; you know the one that just sort of glows," she said as if to give me a cooking tip.
"Yes, I suppose it is," I replied, not having the faintest idea of the tip she was giving me.

I was fifteen or so years older than Pearl and yet it was as if I was a young child, back in the room where I had learned so much at my mother's knee. I certainly was learning things about the 1960s way of life. To avoid sounding too stupid I decided that the best policy was to ask as little as possible.

The toast was then removed and turned around for the other side. I imagined it was quite a warm job doing toast like that but with today's weather quite a pleasant one. I noticed that Pearl's hand had become quite red with the heat. She probably didn't have the myriad of lotions that I owned, but there again you wouldn't find me putting my hands so close to the flames.

"Well what am I like!" she exclaimed "Sometimes I don't know if I am on this earth or Fullers! I've left the butter in the pantry." Off she trotted once more.

I was halfway through eating my toast when two things happened. Pearl was doing a second slice of toast for herself or Harry when through the window we saw the arrival of the ambulance. It was a strange looking vehicle but I had seen something similar on the TV in an old re-run of a series called 'Heartbeat'. Its arrival coincided with the return of John.

"The O'Rourkes were all out so I had to run to the shops. It's hard going on all that snow and ice. I finished up on my backside twice!" His demeanour then changed from jovial to very serious. "Have you seen what's just arrived at the gate?"
"Yes," said his Mother, "it's the ambulance for Eva. It's strange that you have the same name as my mother. She is not very well at present so she has moved in with us. It does make life difficult for everyone with three generations under the same roof, but we get by."

"No Mum, look behind the ambulance. There's a police car and that looks like PC Evans getting out of it."
I didn't quite know whether he was concerned for me or himself.

"I will explain everything to PC Evans. There is no need to worry, John."
"Thanks but it won't be easy."
"What have you done wrong John?"

It was at this point that I realized that John might not have told his mother everything about the previous night's goings on.

"He's done nothing wrong Pearl. He helped an old lady out of a difficult situation and did the best he could."

There was a knock at the side door, and Pearl went to answer it.
"She's in here."
Pearl re-entered with two middle-aged ambulance men.
"We have been instructed to take her to Hightown Hospital but the police want to talk to her first."
Pearl started to protest. "She's not well enough to talk to the police!"
"It's OK Pearl. They just need to ask me some questions. Have you a wheelchair or something to help me into the ambulance," I addressed the two men."
"Yes, we'll fetch it in."

Eventually, they manoeuvred me into the old battered wheelchair and out of the door.
"I'll come back and see you," I shouted over my shoulder, "when I'm out of hospital. Bye."

PC Evans stood by the gate. He tried to look stern but I felt that he had a degree of sympathy for my plight.
"Thought you'd run away from us, did you?"
"Well 'run' might not be the right word."
"Did those boys help you escape?"
"Of course not! Why would they want to do that? I hardly know them. It was you who fouled up by letting me

escape and not watching over me like you should have done. Wait until I see your superior and let him know just how lax you've been!"

Going on the attack seemed like a good ploy. It took the attention away from the boys and put it firmly in PC Evans' court.

He muttered something about seeing me later, but I had made it clear I was not to be messed with. I had had dealings with many officers of the law in many centuries and I knew my rights probably better than PC Evans.

It started to snow heavily once more. With the fading light and the lights of the cars in the street, the snow glowed in that magical way that it does as it settles against any object that gets in its way. It was the time to be sat in front of a roaring log fire, looking out at that wonderful white wonderland scene but sadly, I wasn't!

Pot luck

It was still snowing when I arrived at the hospital. It took about two hours for me to be assessed and X-rayed, which wasn't too bad. As a child I had once fallen off my bike on a Saturday afternoon and Mum and I had spent four and a half hours in Accident and Emergency with lots of footballers and rugby players.

With the demise of the National Health Service some ten years ago, things had improved for the people who could afford a certain standard of medical care. Now everybody had to pay for medical insurance which provided them with a level of service that they could afford. It was multi-tiered system that favoured the rich and healthy.

The really unusual thing for me about this visit to the hospital, apart from not having to pay, was that my leg had been put in this strange pot-like thing that came half way up my calf and weighed a ton!

Eva and the Winter of 63

I hadn't seen one of these plaster casts for years; probably it had been in some old film. From my limited knowledge I thought that all bone breaks were fused nowadays by some sort of laser machine and the procedure took only minutes.

The doctor said that I had to keep the plaster cast on for six weeks to allow the bone to heal!

I don't know who made the decision, either the doctor or the police, but I was put in what they called a 'ward'. It was given a number, Ward 17 and I was in bed number three. The bed was a really old metal contraption more like the torture racks that I had seen in old horror movies. Gone were the mattresses that moulded into your body to give you a good night's sleep. My mattress felt as if it was made from concrete and had funny little dimples in it which left marks on your skin.

There were about twenty beds in the 'ward' and what was really cute was that each bed had a curtain around it which could be drawn for privacy. The curtain was some kind of plastic I think and wasn't in its 'first flush of youth' either. It was a dirty beige colour.

My curtain was open and standing at the foot of my bed was a middle aged woman and a very young policeman. They say that you know that you are getting old when the policemen start to look young; well this one looked fresh out of 'Huggies'.

The lady with the dark blue uniform spoke to me. "We are going to have to keep you in hospital while we find out where you live."

There was a hint of malice in her voice. The message I got was 'You are too demented to be trusted and are probably on day release from a home somewhere in outer space!'

I smiled and said, "Thank you, nurse."
She scowled, "I'm Matron."
What the heck was a matron?
"Sorry I don't feel too good after my accident." In truth it wasn't the accident that made me feel bad, it was the night in the shed in arctic conditions.

I thought that I had frostbite in my legs but the doctor thought that in time the feeling in my legs would come back.
"Where did you say you lived?" asked the young policeman, "We don't seem to be able to find any record of you anywhere."

It was 'lie-time' again, but what lie would buy me the most time?

"Do you know I can't remember! The accident must have made me lose my memory. I can't really remember how the accident happened. Maybe my memory will come back after a rest. I still feel very cold."

I couldn't see any radiators in the ward, it only seemed to have pipes around the room and definitely no under-floor heating.

Eva and the Winter of 63

"Never mind," said Matron, "just get some rest and I'll get one of the nurses to bring you a cup of hot tea."

Everybody seemed to use the word hot in relation to tea. Every cup I had drunk apart from some Japanese green tea a friend had given to me had been hot unless I had forgotten to drink it for about twenty minutes. It must have been the very cold weather at that time that made people stress the 'hotness' of tea.

"That's very kind of you."
"Visiting time is at seven after tea has been served."

There were about four empty beds as far as I could see. The one to my left was vacant. Lying next to people in an old fashioned dormitory-arrangement was strange. In 2048 each patient had their own room, the size of which depended on the level of medical insurance they had bought.

I wasn't expecting any visitors as I knew no one in 1963 who would have braved the cold and snow to come and see me, but I was wrong. Alan, Derek and his mother Sheila turned up. Of course, the O'Rourkes had a car!

"John is sorry he couldn't come to see you tonight. He had to look after his younger brother Richard because his Mum and Dad have gone to Ackton hospital to visit his Grandad who's been rushed in there," said Derek as they arrived.

We then had an awkward sort of conversation as you do when you are visiting someone who is ill in hospital. Why is it that you never quite know what to say?

The boys brought me grapes probably bought by Sheila. How quaint! Grapes were now banned in hospitals along with flowers and nearly everything else as they were a source of germs and infection. I don't suppose for one moment that the boys and Sheila had had to wash their hands in disinfectant hand gel.

The only conversation of note happened when Sheila went to talk to Matron, and the two boys became animated.

"We'll have to get you out of here and away from this place," Derek said, "I overheard my father talking to PC Evans and they really do believe that you're a dangerous Russian spy."
I smiled. "And how do you propose to do that?" I pointed to the plaster cast that I exposed out of the blankets on my bed.
The boys seemed to blush at the sight of a naked fifty-three year old knee.
"Sorry, I didn't quite mean to do that. I meant to stress the point that it would be really difficult for me to move with this 'pot' on!"

My 'nightdress' wasn't something the boys were used to seeing either. It was a piece of material, open at the back and tied together at the top with a bow.

Eva and the Winter of 63

"Well, we have come up with a plan," said Alan.
"OK let's hear it. The last one didn't quite work, did it?"
Immediately I felt bad about saying that.
"Sorry," I said, "that was uncalled for, as you were only trying to do your best."
"It's OK," said Alan, "it was a daft plan. This one's much better."
"Why are you taking the trouble to do this for me?"
"We feel really guilty about what we did. If it wasn't for us you wouldn't be in hospital."
"True, but it was partly my fault as well."

"How well can you walk?"
"As you can see, not very well with this heavy pot-thing on."
"Let us know when you can walk reasonably well and we shall put our plan into action," continued Derek.
"Aren't you going to tell me what it is?"
"Not for the moment. We have to finalize a few things."
"Keep up with the 'loss of memory' story," said Alan.
"What!" I said in surprise.
"We heard Matron tell Mum that you had lost your memory but we know that you haven't, have you?" questioned Derek.
"No, not quite, except I can't remember what day of the week it is?"

The conclusion, after a brief discussion, was that it was Wednesday, the second of January."
"Do you really come from outer space," said Alan.
"I smiled. "Well, sort of, I guess. Look, Mrs O'Rourke is coming back!"

With the return of Sheila, the animated conversation stopped. They left once a nurse, this time in a green uniform, rang the bell to signal the end of visiting time. All the visitors drifted towards the exit, their 'worthwhile job' done for another day.

Plan for escape?

I didn't have any more visitors for a couple of days. The food was as I expected; not quite the cuisine of all those cookery programmes that I had seen so many times on television and Internet screens.

It snowed heavily for the next two days and on the morning of Saturday 5th January the snow stopped for a time.

That afternoon the three boys turned up at visiting time. They had come by bus, which by all accounts had been quite an eventful and exciting journey.
"The bus slid all over the road coming down 'Boot Hill'," said Alan enthusiastically.

The conversation had some very mundane topics, such as the fact they were due to start school again on Tuesday provided the two buses they took could get them there; John had meant to have a date with his girlfriend Val but she didn't turn up because of the heavy snowfall; John's Grandad was a little better but was still in hospital; they had all been involved in snowball fights and watched the ten-pin bowling championships on TV.

All the time, I felt that the main topic of conversation was yet to come. It finally arrived.

"Can you walk OK yet?" asked Derek.
"I can limp along I guess. Why?"
"Our plan is nearly complete, but all this snow and very cold weather means that we have a problem."
"Surely all this snow and ice will clear up soon?"
"The weather forecast says that it's going to be at least the end of January before it does," Derek said in a very matter of fact way.

"I will be able to walk by then."
"Yes but you might be in prison by then," said Alan dramatically.
"I don't think so."
"But we do, Eva," emphasised John "Derek's Dad reckons that you will be arrested and tried as a spy."

"What evidence do they have?"
The boys looked at each other as if deciding who should break the bad news.
"Dad says that they have found some devices in your possessions."
"What devices?"
"They're not sure what they are but they say that they're used for spying purposes."

Eva and the Winter of 63

I started to think about what I had had on me when the collision occurred; not much to be fair. I had gone stocked with cigarettes but little else. I had my purse, a handkerchief maybe and my mobile phone. I guess it was the latter that they thought was the 'spying device'. I bet that the police (or whoever) were having a great deal of fun trying to work out how my mobile phone operated!

"Dad says they can't find out where you live. The address that they have for you is an old church at Three Lane Ends."
"Is there anything that you want to tell us, Eva?" asked John.
"No, the less you know the better. Do you still want to help me?"
"Yes, of course," Alan said, always the first with enthusiasm.
"Well if you can get me to that old church at Three Lane Ends then that would be really helpful."

"None of us can drive as yet," explained Alan.
"It probably has to be by bus then. You said that you had a plan to get me out of here before they lock me up!"
"It needs you to walk properly," repeated Derek, "but according to the doctor that's six weeks away."
"We do have a friend who's a nurse and she could get a wheelchair," said John.

"OK, what's the plan?" I said.
"Well, next Saturday the scout group that we are members of are having a 'bob-a-job' day at this hospital. They are going to let us do jobs for patients

and visitors for a shilling a job. Things like cleaning cars and ambulances, and taking patients for a walk around the hospital grounds."

I hadn't a clue what 'bob-a-job' meant or what a shilling was but I let Derek continue with the plan.
"The idea is to walk you around the hospital gardens and then lead you through a hedge at the back, that leads to Saville Park Sports ground and from there to the bus stop at All Saints Church. We need some clothes for you to wear. Alan can 'borrow' some from his mother. She's about your size. Both the other mums are too small."

I let the potential insult pass. "Where would I change into these clothes, Derek?"
"In the Sports Club changing rooms! A mate of Alan's works there, so we should have no problem getting in."

The boys left as the nurse rang the bell yet again signifying the end of visiting time.

Sadly, I had three more 'visitors' later that day, PC Evans and two who I would term as plain-clothes policemen. They introduced themselves as Detective Inspectors Rosebury and Bowers. I couldn't help but smile, which brought a stern look from DI Rosebury.

"We have a number of serious questions to ask you," he said rather pompously.
"Ask away!"
"We cannot find any record of you anywhere. We've scrutinised the documents that we've found amongst

Eva and the Winter of 63

your possessions but based on these you and your address don't exist."

He produced a number of store cards, bank cards and my business cards from my purse including my photo-ID for my Driving Ability Certificate which weren't introduced until the late 2030s. The shortage of oil and awkwardness of using electricity for cars had meant that there had been a fundamental change in the way people had begun to travel around. Jet packs had been talked about for years so the Government had issued Certificates to show the ability of the person to drive the various modes of transport. Strict tests were put in place to assess the ability of a person for personal travel methods. I had a grade B certificate which did not allow me to carry passengers with my jet propelled transport.

"What actually are these?" he enquired.
"Look, if I told you the actual truth you would not believe me."
"Try us!"
"OK. I was born in the year 1995." It was a tester. They looked at each other then back at me.
"Look at the dates on those cards. What do you think the dates are on those cards?"

DI Rosebury examined the cards that surely he had done several times before.

"What do you think '09/48' means on that dark blue card that you have in your hand? There's my Driving Ability Certificate. The date it expires is '04/56'. Any idea what that could mean?"

My sarcasm was getting a bit out of hand but I was fed up with all this 'potential Russian spy' nonsense. They looked confused. Rosebury passed the two cards to DI Bowers and then finally they were handed to PC Evans.

"OK, so they are futuristic dates but that doesn't mean a thing. These could be made up as part of a disguise."
"Have you ever seen cards that look anything like those, DI Rosebury?"
"No, as a matter of fact I haven't. What exactly are they?"
"They are Computer Controlled Cards or CCCs as we call them. They allow us to make transactions from banks and retail outlets."

I tried to keep it as simple as possible but could see from the looks on their faces that they were struggling to understand what I was saying. I realized that some of the words that I was using were alien to them. There was no point in deliberately antagonising them too much.

"Computer Controlled Cards?"
"They're a form of BAC."
Three blank faces stared back at me.
"Sorry. BAC stands for Buy Anything Card. They allow us to do all our transactions with that micro-chip and the devices that read them." Surely they had heard of micro-chips. They had been around for decades in one form or another, even when I was a small girl.

The look on their faces did not change. I tried again.
"I think that they were invented in the 1980s or was it the 90s? They came from the USA."

Eva and the Winter of 63

There was a moment's pause, during which I searched for other ways of convincing them that I was a time-traveller and not a Russian spy.

"These time-travel stories are just plain lies," interjected DI Bowers as if he had had enough of my excuses. "How do you account for this spying device?" He placed his hand in his pocket and pulled out my mobile phone.

"It's not anything to do with spying. It's a phone! I carry it around everywhere with me so I can speak to anybody I wish to. Don't you have them to talk to each other when you are away from the Police Station?"

"Not like this. It's too small to be a phone. The 'lab boys' say it must be some kind of small camera with some kind of signalling device. They reckon the camera is used for taking pictures of documents."
"Yes, it can take pictures. I'll show you if you want."
"You said it was a phone. Phones cannot take pictures."
"There are lots of things I can do on this phone. It plays music, can be a television screen and I can get emails on it and search the Web."

It was clear that I had gone too far for DI Bowers.
"Eva . . ." he stalled for a moment, "whatever your name is."
DI Rosebury helped him out, "Eva Mills it says on these cards.
"Eva Mills," DI Bowers repeated, "I am arresting you on the suspicion of spying for the Russians. You have the right to remain silent but anything that you do say may be taken down and used in evidence against you. Do you understand?"

"Yes, I understand." I said resignedly.
"We are putting a twenty-four hour guard on you and when you are able to walk, we will take you down to the police station to be formally interviewed by Special Branch detectives from London."

"I can only tell them what I have told you, which is the truth. I can travel in time and was born in 1995 and have come here from 2048."
"Yes, yes we've heard all that nonsense. Time-travel is for films and books and not the real world."

There was no use in me arguing. They had made up their minds. I remembered that poor John had suffered the same sort of disbelief when we returned from our first adventure in the 17th century with the young child Valentine. He was found guilty of kidnapping me and Valentine and was about to be sent down when I rescued him.

The two detectives turned and left the ward, leaving poor PC Evans to do the first stint of 'night-guarding' the 'dangerous spy'! It looked as if with me being guarded day and night, Derek's plan would be a non-starter. I settled down for another uncomfortable night on the 'bed from hell'.

The boys made another visit on Monday afternoon, the day before they started school. I told them the bad news as quietly as I could, away from the young PC who was sitting on a chair at the end of my bed. The string of PCs assigned to guard me had been a source of great amusement. They sat impassively as they were tormented and flirted with in equal measure by some of the more mature women on the ward.

It must have been difficult for the young PCs to pass the night away with all the sounds that nearly twenty women made during their sleep. Their only comfort was that there were some young attractive nurses on duty, but sadly for them, they were under the watchful eye of the Matron.

The boys looked disappointed that all their carefully laid plans had come to nothing.
"There must be a way of getting rid of the policeman on Saturday. Can't you think of something Eva?" said Alan.
"I'll try. It seems a shame to waste all the hard work that you boys have put in. What have you been doing today?"

"We've been around town and bought some records."
"Which ones?" I enquired.
"The latest Elvis record, 'Return to Sender', it has been at number one for a few weeks, and 'Dance On' which is the new one from The Shadows. Do you know them?" John asked.

I could hardly tell them that the only thing I knew about Elvis Presley was that he was dead. I was pretty sure The Shadows must have been too.

"I'm a bit too old for all these new songs."
"I thought all the 'old dears' liked Cliff Richard and The Shadows." Alan, as seemed his custom, put both feet where his mouth should have been.

"Eva's not an 'old dear'," protested John, "she's only as old as my Mum."

Even at my age I still loved compliments and this certainly was one!
"But your Mum likes Cliff Richard and The Shadows," Alan was not going down without a fight.
"I am a bit older than your Mum, John," I confessed.
"What's the weather like today?" I said, trying to change the subject.

"The weather is still freezing but there's been no further snow today. I had to go and get some paraffin for Nanna Eva's paraffin heater. Some nights the windows freeze up on the inside so we have to keep her bedroom as warm as possible. With Grandad now in hospital, she has to sleep alone. She's still not very well. Mum says that she has jaundice."

I felt inwardly sad since jaundice was quite often a forerunner of death from cancer.

They left me before the end of visiting time as Alan and John had to meet their girl friends at 5.30pm and Derek had a piano lesson!

My ankle was still painful so there was no real problem in convincing the medical staff that I wasn't well enough to visit any police station.

Eva and the Winter of 63

The problem was still there however. If I was to escape from the hospital without anyone noticing and go into hiding for six weeks whilst my ankle mended, I needed a diversionary tactic to remove whichever PC was guarding me next Saturday. It had dawned on me fairly early on that I couldn't really go back to 2048 with a 1960s pot on my ankle. It would take a lot of explaining to my family never mind any medical practitioner. To take the pot off now could possibly result in problems for the rest of my life. At least a spell in a prison on suspicion of being a spy wouldn't be too long, would it?

Several ideas on how to divert the PC went through my head. Most of them were of the 'romantic-diversion' type, involving one of the nurses to act as some kind of decoy. Talking a nurse into trying to help me escape might get them into trouble or they could just 'grass' on me.

The solution when it came was much simpler. In 2048 I would have been guarded by a female law enforcement officer, but in 1963 I was being guarded totally by the male variety and where can males not go? The ladies' toilets!

Maybe he could stand guard on the door to the toilet but for the past few days very few of them had had the courage to follow me there. They just had to let me get on with it. What I must do over the next few days until Saturday 12th January was to deliberately lengthen the time it took me to go!

The next few days were, judging from my view through the window, extremely cold. The windows were not double glazed and therefore were a constant source of cold and condensation.

According to the TV weather forecasts which we could only watch in the evenings, there looked to be no let-up in the severe arctic conditions for some time. One other strange thing about 1963 was that there were no day-time television programmes, so evenings from about 6pm onwards were the only viewing times. What did they do with young children during the day!

Each bed had its own set of earphones in order for us to listen to the radio and television, so that the sound did not interfere with the riveting conversations that the visitors were having with their loved ones.

I was awoken at about 7.30am on the Saturday morning and offered breakfast. Since I had no idea when I would be eating next, I decided to eat as much cereal and toast as I could. I opted for porridge. I doubted whether the boys would have thought through all the ramifications of my escape and food might be the one thing that they had not thought about. I was seriously worried about their involvement. I could see the excitement that they might get from aiding a fugitive on the run but if we got caught it might leave them with blemishes on their records which could have life-changing consequences.

The hospital had allowed the Scout group to earn their 'bob a job' money in the morning rather than disrupt visiting time later in the day.

Eva and the Winter of 63

The guard who came on duty at 8am was one of the nicer, less pretentious, PCs. His name was PC Graham Cross, and old Mrs Ironside, who was in the next bed to me, knew Graham's mother as they were neighbours.

"Fancy being paid to look after this young lady," she had once said, as if to embarrass him. "Do you know Eva, I remember Graham when he was in nappies. A real cutie he was."

PC Cross inevitably went slightly red and usually at the end of her story made a trip to somewhere off the main ward to relieve his embarrassment.

I wondered if I could encourage Mrs Ironside or Betty, as she was better known, to go down memory lane just one more time as I left for the toilets. This just might keep him occupied a little longer so I had a little more time for my escape.

I had been given a very old wooden walking stick to get around with; hardly the 'high-tech' thing that I had seen in modern-day hospitals. Each person with a walking problem got their own little one-seater buggy. I am not sure that they helped a great deal in the healing process but were wonderful to get around in.

The Scouts began to arrive at about 10.30am and out of the corner of my eye I saw the three boys arrive, all smartly dressed in their khaki shirts, grey trousers and funny things around their necks. Their shirts displayed badges, presumably indicating all their achievements in the Scouting movement.

I began to say my rehearsed lines to Betty, just loud enough for anyone who was bored and might want to hear and have some fun at PC Cross' expense.

"Did you ever see PC Cross in a tin bath when he was little, Betty?" I had found out a bit about tin baths and the stories that emanated from them from a previous visit to the 1950s on one of my collecting expeditions.

"Oh yes, he was ever so cute," she repeated predictably and then launched into a story about him not liking water and soap getting into his eyes.

"I'm just going to the toilet," I whispered to PC Cross as I passed him, "it's urgent but I won't be long." He gave me a half smile and then returned his attention to Betty's story and how he could presumably limit the damage to his reputation.

The story would take five minutes at least. Betty's stories would often weave their way slowly forward and then backwards as her memory remembered something that she thought was important but not necessarily relevant to the story that she was telling.

As I turned to look back at her, there was quite a group now gathering, intently listening to the tale of a very young PC Cross and his bath-time experiences. There was no way PC Cross dare leave whilst the story was being told by such an important figure as Betty Ironside!

There was quite a surprise awaiting me as I hobbled to the entrance to the ward. The toilets were to the right, next to the restrooms and the nurses' and matron's offices were to the left, but standing behind the three boys was a wheelchair. OK it wasn't one of the modern types which you need a Driving Ability Certificate to drive, but it was a welcome sight. They even had had the foresight to provide a blanket!

They smiled and Derek spoke, "would you like a 'bob a job' walk missus?"
"Why yes, that would be nice."
A nurse came out of the offices, somewhat in a hurry, carrying a metal pan.
"Is it OK if we take this lady for a 'bob a job' walk?" Derek assumed control.
"Yes, of course," she said in a harassed voice and rushed onto the ward on her mission of mercy.

Soon I was being pushed towards the hole in the hedge at the furthest point of the hospital grounds. Once through the hole we were in a sports ground with a very rough-looking track made up of what looked like rough stones. It was nothing like the modern day track that I had taken my children to on this very same piece of ground. The changing rooms too were very different. They just consisted of metal hooks on a wooden board with wooden seats.

The boys had had the decency not to come in with me but to stand on 'look-out' duty. In truth I could have done with their help. They had, for boys, been very sensible in their choice of Alan's Mum's clothes.

Eventually, I managed to put on an over-sized bra and pants, a purple blouse, a red cardigan and a white skirt. It was quite a combination and not necessarily the colour scheme I would have gone for if it had been my choice. However, the clothes did fit me, which is more than I could say for the shoes. I wasn't too sure why the boys had given me two shoes as the 'pot' made shoe wearing impossible but even the right shoe that I could wear was a size or so too big.

In more ways than one, I hobbled out to meet the boys and was very relieved to sit once more in the chair and be pushed towards the exit to the sports ground.
"We'd better move quickly, the bus is due soon," said John.
"What exactly is your plan now?"
"Better than the last one!" John quipped.
"Yes, it wasn't that well thought out was it?" remarked Alan.
"To be fair, you didn't have much time to think it through."

"We'd better get a move on before they miss you. We'll tell you our plans once we're on the bus and away from any danger of being discovered."

The bus stop was just outside the church. It was a nervous time waiting for the bus to arrive. At any moment the 'balloon' might go up and all hell might break loose.

"Where are we going?"
"We're waiting for the Leeds bus."
"Are we going to Leeds?"

Eva and the Winter of 63

"No, not quite. Here's the bus," said Derek.
"What do we do with the chair?"
"It folds up a little and we can take it on board with us. Are you OK to climb on the bus?" John enquired.
"Yes, I think so. I haven't been on a bus for years and it's a double-decker."
The boys seemed a little amused at my enthusiasm. I could only assume that they travelled on buses every day of their lives. For me it was a treat.

"Can we go upstairs?"
"I don't think that would be a good idea with that pot on your leg, do you?"
"What an idiot. I must be feeling better. No, you're right John, downstairs it is. What about buying the tickets? Do you have passes?"

They smiled and Alan said, "The conductor will be here in a minute and we'll need to pay him for an adult and three children to Three Lane Ends."

They must have thought 'what a batty old lady!' but I was genuinely excited at the prospect of the journey.
"But I haven't got any money! The police have all my possessions including my wallet."
"Not to worry," replied Derek, "we've thought about that. We'll pay for the trip and maybe you can pay us later."
"By getting us a gun each!" The other two looked at Alan and he apologised.

In short, the plan was simple. With poor Nanna Eva ill in John's home in Ferry Fryston and Tom her husband in hospital, their house was empty at least for the time being. John had 'borrowed' the key from his Mother and Father and it would be my safe haven for at least a few days.

"Mum may come down by bus to make sure that the house is clean but in this weather and with her Mum and Dad to look after, it won't be for a while," John informed us.
"Do you trust me not to steal things?"
"Funny that. I'm not usually a trusting sort of person but for some reason I can't explain, I trust you Eva."

"Well, thank you young man."
He smiled as I had seen him do so many times before. We got off the bus at the appropriate stop and this time it was Alan's turn to do the pushing. After only about twenty metres we turned into a street which the sign announced was Woodview Avenue and stopped.

"We need to be careful that no one sees us enter, so I'll go around and unlock the back door whilst you two take Eva for a short walk up the street. As a sign, I will draw back the upstairs curtains. OK?"
"Which house is it?" asked Derek and Alan in unison.
"I thought that you had both been here before. Number eight, the one with the green door."

We had no idea as to whether we had been seen or not. There were a number of children playing at the top of the street and a man and a woman passed us on the opposite side. On our return journey we saw that John's signal indicated all was well to enter by the path leading to the back door.

Derek opened the gate and we were quickly out of sight at the back of the house. John opened the door and I hobbled in while the other two dealt with the wheelchair-folding routine.

Worries

You may think that my main worry was that I might get caught and put in prison as a spy, or that the boys would get a criminal record for aiding and abetting me to escape. You would be wrong. My main worry was that I hadn't seen a ghost since my accident with the sledge!

It had been, at one time, a real anguish to see so many ghosts. I remember the time on the battlefield at Marston Moor where the sights and sounds of so many spirits were really terrible and had an awful affect on me. OK, so I was only eleven at the time and just coming to terms with my 'special powers' of seeing the dead and moving through time.

But I had been in a hospital and had not seen one dead person walking the ward, neither day nor night. I would have expected to have seen lots of ghosts in a place where, over the years, lots of people had

Eva and the Winter of 63

died. This was really, really worrying me. Had I lost my powers?

Had the blow to my head altered the way I could see people. If I could no longer see the dead, how was I going to return to 2048? I would be stuck in the 1960s, the decade I knew so little about.

8 Woodview Avenue was an end of terrace house with what seemed to be a lawn at the front with a border for flowers, and what looked like the remains of some vegetables which had been grown in the back garden.

I say 'seemed to be' because with all the snow and ice it was difficult to see anything other than the tips protruding above the snow.

I couldn't be certain when the house was built, but to my horror, it had an outside toilet and no bathroom. I felt that I wouldn't be staying here for long, so it would have to suffice for the time being. The back door opened straight into the kitchen. There was no refrigerator, but something John called a 'pantry' in which things could be kept cool. This was not really a problem given the current cold weather.

There was an open fire in the kitchen with what the boys called 'a stove'. I would not have had a clue how to use it, but presumably it was heated from the fire next to it.

John mentioned that since his Grandad Tom was an ex-miner, he got free coal. There was also an open fire in the large living room. The living room had a window looking out over the front garden. The door to the upstairs was at the far end of the room to the right of the window.

At John's suggestion I was to limit my living quarters to downstairs.
"It's very cold upstairs and there's no way of heating it except with hot water bottles in the beds."
The settee was a three seater, so since I wasn't very tall, I could sleep reasonably comfortably on it. It had three cushions on which three people could sit and then there were further embroided cushions laid on it.

The room was deep red in design. The two armchairs and the settee were red, the carpet was red and the flock wall paper was red with white flowers. It certainly wasn't my choice of colour but times and tastes change.

"We have to go now," said Derek, "otherwise our parents will worry. 'Bob a job' only lasts for the morning and early afternoon."

"I'll leave you the key, but before we go let me show you the best places to hide. The outside toilet and shed are out of the question because of the fresh tracks that you would make to get there."
"Does that mean I can't go to the toilet?"
"Ah yes, that is a problem."
"Why don't you be a good Grandson and clear the snow and ice off the path," suggested Alan.
"It will only take a few minutes to clear it all with some shovels," agreed Derek.

Eva and the Winter of 63

"OK, let's do it and hope that no more snow falls."

"Please lock the door once we're gone. The shovels are in the 'coal hole'."
And with that, the boys left to do a 'bob a job' that they wouldn't get paid for. In fact they had not been paid for the first job they did!

I could hear the scraping of metal on the pavement as the snow and ice were cleared. After a few minutes Derek knocked on the kitchen window and they were gone.

The boys had been very thoughtful and I had been impressed by what they had remembered. Not just food and drink, but finding pillows and blankets together with a hot water bottle which John had shown me how to fill with not quite boiling water from the kettle.

"Only fill the bottle half full then press gently on the upper part of the bottle to get rid of the steam and then put the stopper on. It stops it being like a balloon and is easier to put your feet on." John had said in a matter-of-fact way.

It was slightly surprising that he had assumed, quite correctly, that I wouldn't know how to do it. There are many statements I thought I would never utter but then I found myself saying, "Where are you ghosts? Please come and talk to me."

Sadly, no one answered my request as I settled down for a night on a non-metallic bed for the first time in over a week.

In search of Eva Mills

After quite a decent night's sleep given the circumstances, I felt quite refreshed, but the thought of washing in cold water was not appealing.

I refilled my hot water bottle and returned to my bed after eating the breakfast that the boys had left. Not porridge or toast but bread and jam. I managed to make a cup of tea, something I hadn't done for years.

After a slow start, tea and coffee makers had become a real boom industry. The machine had sensors which could recognise not only the words 'tea, coffee, milk, sugar etc' but also recognise the voice of the person ordering it. Being pre-programmed with their individual likes and preferences for making their beverages, the machine did the rest to perfection.

There was an old 'tube-type' television that I had once seen in a museum in York, sitting in the corner of the

Eva and the Winter of 63

living room. It was no use putting it on now as there were no day-time programmes, but I thought that I might risk it later in the evening.

In 2048 televisions could also 'think' for themselves. After recognising the person switching it on, it could offer from the myriad of options, the programmes suited to the person watching. This did lead as ever to family discussions but with many families owning Multiple Internet Screens as they became known, it wasn't a problem.

Suddenly there was a tap on the window. My heart jumped and palpitations started. I peeped from behind the living room door to see John's smiling face.

I opened the back door.

"Just thought I'd pop in to see how you are and bring some more provisions. I have a friend, Brian, who lives further up the street and we're going to do some homework and play a little snooker of course. It's a bit unfair on him though, he's colour blind between red and brown!"

"You do tell him which is which don't you John?"
"Sometimes," he smiled.
"Anyway, I am fine thank you, but would love to wash in hot water. Both taps have cold water in them."

He looked at me in a strange way. "You are funny you know! You can use the kettle to boil some water for washing as well as tea and just mix it with a little cold in the sink."

How stupid of me not to have thought of that. Everything for our washing needs came out of a very well-regulated tap or shower head. Boiling water in a kettle and adding cold water never entered my head. I had got so used to machines doing things for me automatically.

"I could light a fire for you if you want."
I thought of my scary moment with Pearl when the paper caught fire.
"Are you sure you can do it?"
"Of course I can!" he sounded hurt. "Which fire do you want me to light?"
"Perhaps the one in the kitchen is best. People can't see me as they walk past."

He lit the fire in a very professional manner, having got wood from the 'coal hole' as he called it.
"Make sure you bring the wood into the kitchen to dry out before you add it to the fire, otherwise you will get smoke everywhere. I'll fill up the coal scuttle before I go," and he pointed to a strange looking metal cylindrical thing in the hearth.

What wonderful names the 60s had, 'coal hole, scuttle, shovel'.

"John?" I said with some apprehension, "I cannot stay here for long. They are bound to find out how I escaped from the hospital and maybe someone will notice smoke coming from the chimney, or see me through the window."

"Yes, I realize that this was only for a short time."
"I was wondering if you could let me into St James' Church tomorrow? There will be a service today with it being Sunday."

"I'll see what I can do but getting the key might be a problem. Maybe you could look around to see if there are any likely keys here. From memory it's quite a large key. If it isn't here, Grandad must have taken it to our house."

With that, he was gone. I locked the door once more and pondered on whether once inside the church I would be able to see Valentine. If I could it would at least prove to me that I had not lost my 'special powers' even if he was unable to help me out of my present predicament.

Although John was not aware of it, I could remember exactly what the key looked like. He and I had used it in 2008 on our first trip to the 17th century.

At six o'clock I put on the television. I thought I would listen to some programmes as it would pass away a little time and maybe, provided I could keep myself hidden sufficiently, I could probably watch it all evening.

I should have asked John to close the curtains. I daren't do it as I might be seen. Closed curtains in the daytime usually signified that someone in the family had died and I didn't want any neighbours calling to enquire about who had died.

I kept the light off and outside the snow started to fall yet again. I hugged my hot water bottle and settled down to watch the television. The news was just starting.

The items were, as they were in 2048, pretty depressing news; fifty people died when five US helicopters were shot down in the Vietnam War; Congo president placed under house arrest; eight hundred communists arrested in Peru and a military coup in Toga. On a lighter note the 'Mona Lisa' went on show at the National Gallery in Washington and the BBC announced that it was to end its ban on mentioning politics, royalty, religion and sex in its comedy shows. That made me smile given what shows were to follow in the 21st century.

Suddenly, the male news reader said, "We have breaking news. Recent spying scandals have been brought to a head with the escape from a hospital in West Yorkshire of a suspected Russian agent." And there on the screen was a picture of me, obviously taken from my Driving Ability Certificate.

The news reader went on, "The suspect is female, in her mid-fifties, blue eyes, light-coloured hair and most importantly she has a pot on her left foot as a result of breaking her ankle in a previous desperate attempt to escape from the authorities. The police say that the public should not approach this person as she is very

Eva and the Winter of 63

dangerous and most probably is in possession of guns and other weapons. If you see this person please contact your local police station as soon as possible."

I was shocked to say the least and gazed blankly as the news ended and the predictable weather forecast was explained.

They told lies! Why was I surprised at that? It had almost become second nature for news stories to be exaggerated for their salacious and shocking content.

They had taken all six guns from me and they knew it! They were scaring people in their own homes that some dangerous killer was on the loose, but more importantly to me they were scaring them into keeping a lookout for me in and around the West Yorkshire area.

Here in 1963, I was cut off from any immediate contact with anyone. My mobile phone had been confiscated as a Russian spying device. Having a phone and being able to contact people at any time was something that I took for granted in 2048. Although the phone would be little or no use to me now, I still missed not being able to use it to phone, text or email anyone.

I needed to get into that church and check my powers were still intact and then get as far away from here as I could. The problem was that the pot on my leg, which had been emphasised on television, was a dead giveaway if anyone saw me. Mobility was not my strong point at the moment. I desperately needed a ghost!

St James' Mission and the search for Valentine

Even though it was only 5pm, it was very dark when John arrived the following day on his way back from school. The weather remained cold but there had been some sunny periods which had lifted the gloom somewhat.

"We ought to wait a bit before we go to St James'," he suggested. "Are you sure that you will be more comfortable there rather than here?"

"Yes John, I can hide more easily in a church and it might be warmer," I lied. I wanted to be in the church so I could meet a familiar ghost! Of course, I couldn't tell John that.

At about 6 o'clock, John thought it was time to go. On balance he thought it would be better to take the wheelchair. Although it would probably be more conspicuous, it would certainly take less time. We couldn't leave it any later, as John needed to be home.

"I can always tell Mum that I had a Cross Country to do after school. We've had plenty of practises for the Yorkshire Cross Country Championships at Barnsley next month, so she's not to know. My kit's still wet and dirty from the three-mile cross country we had to do in PE this morning."

"It's not good to lie though, best to say nothing unless you're asked."
"I can hardly tell her that I've been to see the dangerous Russian spy of television fame, can I? Do you have any guns?"
"No John, lies all lies."
"Thought as much. Alan still thinks you have concealed one somewhere!"

We left the house and without too much trouble we made it to the front door of the church without incident. John's Grandfather had indeed taken the church key to his daughter's house and John had managed to locate it in Nanna Eva's bedroom.

"I'll give you the key so you can lock yourself in, but I'll take the chair back to the house and be off. You've plenty of blankets and there's a kettle in the vestry for the hot water bottle you have." And off he went.

I looked around that familiar church. Although it had been some time since I had been there, it was 2006 I think, it didn't look too different in its 1960s' state. The church actually got demolished some time around 2008 and the bungalow I currently lived in had replaced it.

Valentine wasn't there in his usual place but there again why should he have been? As a result of my second trip into the 17th century he had a much better reason for staying at his home in Great Staughton Manor near Bedford with his wife Hester.

I settled down on one of the pews and awaited his arrival.

Tuesday morning arrived, but still no Valentine. It was still very cold even with all the blankets and the hot water bottle. The pews were hard but seeing Valentine would solve all my immediate problems! I could use him in several ways. I could go with him back to the 17th century for a while. They knew me well at Great Staughton Manor and I was always made welcome. The pot on my leg, whilst being a talking point, would not be such a big deal as it would be in 2048. It would just be shrugged off as one of the quirky things that Eva did!

I could, with Valentine's help, also go to the place of his death on the battlefield at Marston Moor, near York. I preferred the Great Staughton Manor option!

I stayed at the Mission Church for four long days and nights. According to John, the mid-week services had

Eva and the Winter of 63

been cancelled because of the weather conditions, such was the severity of the weather. He called in a few times with food and drink, and some more of Alan's Mum's clothes. Why wasn't she missing them?

The boys were really resourceful. The police had interviewed all the scouts that had done 'bob a job' on the Saturday of the 'escape', asking if they had seen a middle-aged lady leave the ward during the morning. Fortunately, as yet, no one had put two and two together to realize that three of the boys in the scout troop had had dealings with the lady in question before the escape.

By the following Saturday morning I was really beginning to worry. What if I had lost all my powers of time-travel? What would I do? I didn't want the life of a middle-aged woman in the 1960s. I wouldn't have the opportunities that I had had in the 21st century.

Whilst I was contemplating my situation, the door to the right of the altar suddenly opened and, before I had chance to hide in the vestry, a young man in his twenties I guess, walked into the church.

He completely ignored me and made his way down past the altar to the front pew, where he knelt in prayer. Was this a young rector or curate? But that door he had come through only led to a small room used for Sunday School or further back to the boiler room which heated the church. Nobody as far as I knew ever came into the church from the back door, did they?

I didn't move and tried not to make a sound. He remained in a state of prayer for a few minutes and then got up and made his exit through the door he had entered. I thought about following him but decided against it and awaited the arrival of the boys.

When they did eventually arrive I told them about the young man I had seen. John seemed genuinely surprised. "The Rector is quite old and at the present time we don't have a curate. The last one left for a parish somewhere down south," John explained.

"I need to know who he is, friend or foe."
"You say that he completely ignored you?"
"Yes. Came in, prayed and left!"
"That's very strange," said Derek, "why wasn't he shocked to see you here? I hope that he hasn't gone to the police."
"We need to move you back to the house, there are services in the church tomorrow."

"Can I come back here on Monday?" I asked.
"I don't see why not," replied John.
"Have you had any more visits from the police?"
"No, they seem certain that you have been whisked away by the Russians according to yesterday's news on the television."

I chose my next words carefully. "Do you know if anyone has died recently in the area?" It wasn't careful enough. "You think that the man could be a ghost?" asked Alan. "No Alan, I was thinking that the church might be used for funerals during this week. Could you check please John?"

Eva and the Winter of 63

"Yes of course," replied John obligingly, "it would cause problems if they had a mid-week funeral here."

The man appeared several times during that Saturday, but I chose not to say anything, even though I was now certain that he was a ghost. It would account for the reason why he ignored me as he thought I couldn't see him.

I was moved under the darkness of early evening back to the house where I stayed until Monday evening. By that time, I had made up my mind to approach the young man.

"You were right to ask about a recent death in the area. A man got killed in a road accident outside the church a week last Sunday, but it's OK because the funeral for him is at All Saints' Church in Hightown."

"Do you know the man's name?"
"No sorry, I don't but I could find out for you if you want."
"It's OK now the funeral isn't at St James'."

The man did not appear on the Monday evening, but at about 10am on the Tuesday morning, on what appeared to be the coldest day yet according to the ice on the inside of the church windows, the ritual occurred again. With a degree of apprehension, I spoke to the man.

"Excuse me, can I help you?"
He swung around, eyes open wide in shock.
"You, you can see me?" He stammered.
"Yes, I can see you," and I almost added, "I am so pleased to see you."

"But, I'm dead!" he exclaimed.
"Sorry, what did you say your name was?"
"I didn't but it's Graham Newton. Why can you see me when I'm dead?" he repeated.

"I can see and talk to people who have recently died. It's just a special skill that I have. You are in Limbo before the final decision is made." I decided to make it as 'matter of fact' as I could.
"What final decision?"
"I don't really know. It's just that at some point in the future I won't be able to see you."
"How long will I stay in this Limbo?"
"It varies. Sometimes I have known it be for months."
I hesitated for a moment. "You could really help though."
"How?"

I explained as carefully as I could about the circumstances that I was in and that the police were looking for me as a potential spy.
At the end of the explanation Graham said, "I'm still not sure how I can help you."

"Well, you definitely have scare value."
"I'm not that ugly am I?" he said with a smile.
"No, no of course not, but one of my other skills is that everybody I touch can see what I see. In the past I have

introduced many an unsuspecting troublemaker to some gruesome sights!"
"I've gone from ugly to gruesome now have I?" He laughed.

"You have got a pessimistic streak haven't you?"
"I'm dead! How optimistic do you want me to be?"
"Sorry, being dead does take some getting used to."
"Have you had to deal with many people who are in Limbo?"
"Yes I suppose so."

"I must admit that it's really good to talk to you. It's been a terrible week, being able to see people but not being able to speak to them. I do feel a lot better talking to you."

I was really surprised how well he was taking his death. Maybe there was something he wasn't prepared to tell me. I didn't dare tell him that cheering up ghosts was a by-product of my powers.

"Let me get this straight. When the time comes, you want me to scare a few policemen?"
"It could come to that, if they find out where I'm hiding."
"Could we talk a little more about your knowledge of what happens when somebody dies? And a bit more about those 'corridors of transit' you mentioned? They sound fun."

We talked for quite a time about Valentine and my journeys into the 17th century. I'm not sure what type of person Graham had been in life, but in death, once over the shock, he was a very understanding young man. Unlike many I had met in similar situations, he did not seem bitter about what had happened to him to bring his life to an early end. There was something not quite right about his attitude towards his current position.

"What's the plan?" he asked.
"I haven't got one. I just play it by ear."
"You have to have a plan of escape!"
"Well, my difficulty is this!" I moved the blanket from my left leg to reveal the pot. "This is what is stopping me getting home."
"Oh, I see."
"I'm holed up here in the 1960s for six weeks until this comes off and my ankle is back to normal."

Unexpectedly, he suddenly said, "I like you and I think that we could have some fun together." This didn't seem right.
"You would be great company and at present my only way of possibly escaping capture for a crime that I haven't committed."

"I've had a bit of trouble myself with the law and have been stupid at times. All my own fault, even my death."

I decided not to enquire why that was the case but attempted to cheer him up.
"Graham and Eva fight the Law!" He smiled at my suggestion.
"Can I move around in Limbo?"
"As far as I know, you can go wherever you want."

"How many people will be able to see me?"

"From my experience just me, except that I did meet a lady in 1605 who had the same powers as me."
"You've been as far back as 1605? Will I be able to go back that far?"
"I don't think so. Just back to the date when you were born."
"1941 eh! It was quite an eventful year, with the war and all that."
"Quite a dangerous time to be born!"
"I suppose there were lots of people born like I was when my Dad came home after Dunkirk."

Although that was not a factually accurate statement, I understood what he meant.
"In the future, people who were born in and just after the war become known as 'baby-boomers'."
"That's a strange name."
"Yes it is, but it does give you another way of helping me."
"How?"
"Take me back to 1941 and away from the spy-hunters!"
"I can do that can I?"
"It might be possible but you need to leave Limbo first."
"It is all very complicated but you seem extremely knowledgeable about life after death."

"I do need you to do me one big favour though."
"Name it!"
"I don't want you to appear when the boys who are helping me escape the clutches of the Law are around. I don't want them to know about the powers that I have."

"Why not? I would want to tell everybody!"

"It's a long story but I meet one of the boys again in 2006 and if he found out about my powers now it would change things and I'm not sure what would happen. In all my travels I have tried hard not to alter the course of history."

The weaving of webs

Graham was true to his word and never appeared when the boys brought me fresh provisions of food, drink, clothes and toiletries. I really missed my creams and make-up. I hadn't 'put my face on' for nearly a fortnight.

"They're still after you. You were on the news again last night."

The three boys were all at the same school and with a bit of a detour were able to call in on their way home. Where they hid the provisions, including my 'new' clothes, whilst they were at school was anybody's guess.

I tried hard to keep a track of the days, as I had worked out that my six weeks was up on the 13th February. How I was going to get the pot off was another matter. With the present situation, strolling into any hospital and asking for the pot to be removed seemed to me to be out of the question.

On one of Graham's visits, on what I believed to be Wednesday 23rd January, he had an apprehensive look on his face.
"Eva," he said tentatively, "maybe there is a favour you could do for me."
"Depends on what it is."
"I want to speak to my wife Carole and from what you said you can make it happen."
"Yes, that is true but I have to be in contact with her for her to see and hear you."
I could see that he was troubled and maybe he hadn't thought through what he might say, given the circumstances.
"As I say I could do that, but the difficulty is getting her here or getting us to her."

"I've thought about that. My funeral is on Monday next at All Saints and then at Four Lane Ends Cemetery. Maybe we could see her there."
"It's very risky."
"I need to explain something to her and say how sorry I am."

I didn't enquire as to why he might be sorry for what he had done. At the moment it really wasn't appropriate. He was clearly sad and troubled about something.

This was not the cheerful Graham but one who had had time to think about his plight, perhaps a bit belatedly.

Eva and the Winter of 63

"Of course I want to help you but we have to be very careful not to make matters worse." I wasn't too sure what I meant by that. Could the situation be any worse? I was on the run from the police and Graham was dead!

But I had a foreboding that things could get a whole lot worse.

"Have you any ideas on how we can talk to her?"
"Well, I was wondering if you could get those boys to take you to the cemetery on Monday."
"How far is it?"
"Not far, about a mile."
"It's a long way to push a wheelchair."
"There's a bus that comes from Leeds on its way to Pontefract that goes past the cemetery regularly."
"I'll ask them but I don't want the boys being involved in anything ghostly. Understand?"

For the first time today he smiled. "I understand."

I broached the subject the next time the boys came. They looked at me in surprise.
"Why do you want to risk getting caught by going to a funeral?" asked Derek.
I had thought long and hard about this inevitable question. "It's a dear friend of mine that has died and I don't want to miss the chance to say my last farewell to her."

"It's very risky. We are at school so we really couldn't help you."
"We could 'twag' school," said Alan.
The other two looked at him. "And if we get caught?" John was being very cautious.
"Have you ever taken a risk for someone, John," Alan wasn't finished.
John looked at Derek for support. He shrugged.
"We could give it a go I suppose," and it was left at that for the time being.

There must have been something complex about Graham's death as he informed me that the funeral on Monday would have been over two weeks since the day he died.

I did now have some time to think about the downside to Graham's plans. I could tell that he was desperate to talk to his wife, although he never told me why. The plain truth was that if he was to help me, I needed to help him.

The weather, if it was possible, had got colder. The boys had had to take me back to the house on a number of occasions because of services at the church and a beetle drive (whatever that was!). The church had a dual purpose; it was a place of worship and a place to socialise.

Reluctantly the boys devised a plan to 'twag' school for the morning of the funeral and instead of going to school they caught the bus to Three Lane Ends and St James'. As Graham had said the cemetery was about a mile or so from St James' but that mile was up a very steep hill. The boys would have really struggled in pushing me all that way.

The bus for the cemetery, according to Alan, was due to arrive at 9.50am, this would mean arriving at the cemetery at 9.55am and a best estimate of when the burial would take place was at about 10.30am. This left us some time to kill, so to speak.

My problem was clear to me. I was there for Graham and what he wanted but had to pretend to the boys that I was there for the funeral of a dear friend.

I did finally manage to convince the boys that, once they had got me to the cemetery, they could get on their way to school and just pretend that the bus had got held up because of the adverse weather conditions. They were reluctant but finally agreed. Of course this meant that we didn't need the antiquated wheelchair and I could hobble the fifty or so metres back to the bus stop once the funeral was over.

We did have a discussion about the fact that not all of the three boys needed to be involved in the trip to the cemetery. But Alan's logic concerning the fact that they would be on the same delayed bus meant that all of them had to be involved.

There was a sort of 'all for one and one for all' spirit amongst my 'Three Musketeers'.

Graham's and Bessie's funeral

I had to invent a name for my friend and, although there was no clear reason why, Bessie came to mind. Probably from an old school saying of mine, 'this is my bessie mate'. On such things are decisions made! I wasn't absolutely sure that it was a name from the 60s, but that is the name I told the boys. The one thing that I didn't tell the boys was that at that bus stop there were five of us and not four, although one would be a non-paying passenger.

Graham sat some distance away from us on the bus which I was pleased was ten minutes late, since it took a lot longer to walk to the bus stop than I had imagined.

He smiled at me for reassurance as we got off the bus. I was very careful not to touch anybody, otherwise Graham would have suddenly appeared to them and all hell would have broken loose.

Eva and the Winter of 63

Once in the cemetery the boys reluctantly left. They were three 'nice' lads who genuinely cared for my well-being at a time when the elderly were held in higher regard than in 2048.

Graham and I stood some distance from the mound of earth that signified where his grave had been dug. The funeral cortege arrived just before 10.30am. There was a long stream of cars that entered the cemetery. Normally, the cemetery was close to the church and people could walk, but in this case the distance from the church of All Saints to the cemetery was nearly a mile.

Some cars parked up whilst the hearse and two other black limousines continued up the gravel roadway to come to rest close by the mound of earth with its green carpet for camouflage.

A very pretty young girl, possibly still only a teenager, and if my eyes didn't deceive me, it was a very pretty pregnant young teenager who got out of the first limousine.

I looked at Graham. He was crying and I then understood why he was so keen to see his wife for one last time.

I had already had an experience of being with someone at their own funeral. It was that of Jon Stow back in 1605. That had been a more jovial occasion or at least that's how it turned out. Jon and his wife Anne were really pleased that they both could be at his eventful funeral. This funeral was, however, quite different.

Graham and I had talked about how we could isolate Carole at the cemetery, but no plan was perfect. Carole would not know who I was and would be a little reluctant to let me touch her.

Graham and I watched as his coffin was lowered into the grave and the mourners stood as the Rector said a final prayer.
"It's strange," Graham whispered as if someone else could hear him, "I've never been a church-goer or religious for that matter, but this is very touching." He wiped his eyes.

"We need to walk closer to the limousine. I'll talk to the drivers," I said.

I walked slowly down one of the gravel paths and turned on to the one behind the row of black limousines. The drivers of the three vehicles were quietly talking as I approached, still hobbling a little.

"Whose funeral is this?"
"Some poor kid who got killed in a car chase. He's left a lovely young widow who's close to giving birth. What an idiot!"

Graham had been walking a few metres behind and hopefully out of earshot.

What happened next was all too predictable. I had been here many times before. As Graham's wife, Carole, came towards the limousine, I approached her to offer my condolences and touched her on the arm, in the way we women do, to show that I understood her grief.

She looked at me, and then looked past me to where Graham stood, screamed and fainted before Graham could say a word.

The sight of a loved one who had just supposedly died brought this reaction. It had been the same with Hester, Anne Stow and all the other grieving widows that I had encountered on my travels.

What followed Carole's scream and faint was not so predictable.

"That's the woman who's wanted for spying," someone shouted. One of the drivers grabbed me and I struggled but he held me firm.
"Are you sure it's her?" came another voice.
"They say that she has a pot on her leg," and before I had the chance to reply he pulled open my coat to reveal the pot. That gave me a glimmer of a chance to escape.

Graham was behind me, in what I assumed was a disturbed state at witnessing the scene. I pulled away out of the clutches of the driver and hobbled as fast as I could towards Graham.

That familiar bright light was a comforting sight as I went down the 'corridor of transit'.

Déjà vue

The droplets of blood fell onto the frozen snow. They fell at regular intervals and as they hit the hard frozen surface they threw out a red ring of smaller droplets, much like the effect of a firework in the sky.

I wiped my hand across my face. Yes, it was my blood dripping as regularly as the beats of a metronome.

I was back again in a familiar position at the bottom of the sledging hill, on all fours staring at the ever-increasing pool of blood. How in heaven's name had I got back to here? Surely Graham's 'corridor of transit' would not take him here as his place of birth?

My thoughts were interrupted by the sudden appearance of two boys that I knew were teenagers. I also knew that they were called Alan and Derek. This was déjà vue. I had gone back in time but only by a few weeks.

Eva and the Winter of 63

I looked around and sure enough there stood Graham. He looked as puzzled as I felt. Just what had happened! One minute we were in the cemetery at Four Lane Ends and the next back here with Alan and Derek and that damned sledge.

"We are ever so sorry missus," said Derek.
"You suddenly just appeared from nowhere and we couldn't get out of your way!" said Alan.

"Yes, yes," I felt like saying, "I know all about what's happened. You have just broken my left ankle again!"

And boy did it hurt. It seemed so much more painful than the first time. It was no use trying to stand up, for as before being on all fours was the best position for me, despite the continual loss of blood from my nose.

As had happened before the younger boy, Alan offered me a handkerchief to stem the flow of blood. Once again, I hesitated for a moment and then graciously accepted the offer, germs and all.

"Go fetch your father Derek!" I said in an unkind manner.
"How, how do you know my name's Derek," he stammered.
"I know your mother Sheila. Now go and fetch your Dad so I can get to hospital to mend this broken ankle."

Still looking a little bewildered, he ran off home.
"You're Alan aren't you?"
"Yes," he said nervously, thinking that he was in deep trouble.

"My name is Eva. Pleased to meet you again!"

"I think this is the bag you were carrying when we hit you."
And before I could stop him, he picked it up and placed it a little closer to where I was now sitting. Just as before, the bag toppled sideways and a gun fell out.

It got the same reaction as Alan looked shocked that in his terms, an old lady wandering around on a dark early evening should possess a gun.

Derek returned with his father who again introduced himself as Michael O'Rourke.
"I'm Eva," I said apologetically, "I'm sorry to have caused you so much trouble."
"I have told Derek a hundred times that using this hill as a sledge run is dangerous. These pathways have been covered in snow and ice for weeks."

Again, Derek looked dutifully admonished but repeated, "She just appeared from nowhere," which although it would seem unlikely to his father, was most definitely the truth.

Once again, Alan tried to help his friend.
"She wasn't there when we started at the top of the hill, we checked, then suddenly, half-way down, bang we hit her!"

The look of disbelief was there again on Michael's face.

I looked across at Graham. "What's going on, Eva?" he shouted.

Eva and the Winter of 63

I couldn't reply. Although I alone could hear what Graham had said, everybody could hear what I was saying, and before I knew it Alan came out with his attack or was it a defence.

"She's got a gun!" He bent down and picked up the one that had fallen out of my bag and was half-hidden in the snow.

As before, Michael and Derek looked a bit taken aback by Alan's revelation.

Again I tried to explain, "I own an antique shop in the town and the guns in that bag are just replicas. I have bought them from a friend in St Andrew's Road. I was on my way to get the bus back to town when the accident happened."

It was still the best I could do.
"Let's get you into the warm and see what damage the boys have done to your ankle and face."
"The face is OK but my ankle is broken," I muttered under my breath. With Michael's and Derek's help, I hobbled the hundred or so metres to their familiar house.

John and PC Evans arrived once again, but I did manage to get a quick word with Graham as he followed us into the house.
"I really don't know what has happened. We have gone back in time about three weeks. It's New Year's Day but we are still in the same area."

He gave me a funny smile, as if demented, "I know," he said, "it's great!" I couldn't really speak to him much after that. I had to go through my interview with PC Evans and persevere another extremely cold night in John's shed.

Graham's story

The only difference in my second night's stay in arctic conditions in the shed was that this time Graham was with me, and I found out for the first time that ghosts don't feel the cold!

The sleep that I got that night was just as bad as the one before, but talking to Graham helped. He told me that he had been a very troubled teenager with little parental control. Alcohol-fuelled binges combined with no job had left him in a situation that had nearly brought him a prison sentence. For what, he wouldn't tell me. His life changed when he met Carole who was working at Woolworths in the town. She was only seventeen at the time. They had 'courted' each other and then two years later had married after they had found out that she was pregnant.

"So what happened to cause your death?" I said bluntly.

He hesitated and it was clear that he was reluctant to tell me.
"I did something stupid."
I waited for some elaboration, but it didn't come.
"Could you help me change what happened?" he eventually asked.
"I wouldn't think so, but if you don't tell me what happened then I can't decide.

Again, he hesitated.
"Look," I said, "I need to get some sleep, so have a think about it, I need the truth mind. I am not stupid remember."
"No, of course you're not! The problem is that I probably deserved to die. I did something that I am ashamed of and let Carole down badly. If she hadn't have fainted she would have probably hit me. She must hate me so much now."

"This really isn't getting us anywhere."
He left me alone so that I could get some rest.

I didn't see him again until I was in hospital after the pot had been applied to my leg. It must have been on the Wednesday morning of the 9th January.

"I've decided to tell you everything," he whispered, still not quite understanding that no-one but me could hear him.
"Ok, I'm listening," I whispered back.

"Carole and I had an argument on the Saturday morning about something stupid. I can't even remember what it was about, it was that trivial. We both said things that we regretted but I left and went to the pub." He hesitated.

"A couple of pints of beer wouldn't kill you, would it?" I prompted quietly.

"No, but it was possibly the reason for what I did next."

"Which was what?"

"I met a girl."

"And Carole found out?"

"No, I told her in anger the next day on the Sunday."

"What did she say?"

"She threw me out. Not literally because she was eight months pregnant, but she started to pack my clothes in a suitcase."

"And what did you do?"

Again there was a hesitation and he started to cry.

"I hit her and stormed out, back to the pub."

After a few moments he said, "I really do love her. She changed my life around; I had got a job, left all the mates who were such a bad influence on my life, no more petty thieving and getting into fights. I really had changed, and now we are having our baby which would have meant such a joy to our lives. And then I went and did something so stupid and she didn't want to know me."

"What do you think I can do to help?" I asked.

"Stop me from dying?"

"You haven't told me what you did."

"I drank too much at the pub again on the Sunday lunchtime and evening. The rest is a bit of a blur but I must have stolen a car late that evening for a laugh, egged on by my mates. Next thing I am being chased by police cars and as I came down through the Potteries, I swerved to avoid something and hit a lamp post."

"What can I do? Stop you drinking? Stop you stealing? Stop you hitting your wife?" I hissed, so much so that people looked at me from the neighbouring beds.

I smiled as if I had been talking to myself.
"I've been thinking about that. If you go to the Rising Sun pub on Saturday night you can talk to me and then I won't bump into that blonde."
"Do you think that you would talk to a middle-aged lady?"
"It would only take seconds for you to delay me and then I wouldn't see her as I went to the loo. If I don't meet her, Carole doesn't throw me out, I don't go to the pub on Sunday and get drunk and steal a car and what's more, I don't die! It's that simple!"

"I don't alter the course of history!" I hissed again, and got even more dirty looks from those around me.
"Yes, you do! Maybe not in a big way like with the 'Gun Powder Plot' and the battle in the Civil War which you told me about, but in small ways you have."

I thought for a moment and yes, he was right! In 1605 whilst trying to return Valentine to his mother, Hester, I had had a big effect on the lives of Rebecca and her two children, Charlotte and Jacob. I had met them at Hampton Court and they had travelled with me to Oxford. I had even brought them into the year 2008 with me, but Rebecca had chosen to return to 1605. But what I had never done was to change history so that someone would escape the clutches of their appointed death. And did I really want to even try to do this for a man who had treated his new wife so appallingly?

Death defying decisions

It dawned on me early in my deliberations about altering history that if I were to stop Graham from being killed I wouldn't in fact meet him in the church. So how would that work? It was a real 'catch twenty-two' situation!

Also the problem was that if I didn't meet Graham, he couldn't help me escape from 1963 and my pursuing spy-catchers. I had a few days still to contemplate what I could do. Personally, I could do nothing to have an effect on the events that led to Graham's death. I was in hospital with little mobility and a policeman watching over me.

On my next meeting with Graham, he seemed very agitated and annoyed with me that I had not come up with a plan to save him. I explained my predicament to him but he wasn't happy.
"You can find another to ghost to help you, can't you?"

Eva and the Winter of 63

"Well, I suppose I could. Have you met any other ghosts on your travels?"
"How would I know? Everybody looks the same to me. Like you I can see everybody, dead or alive."

"Answer me one question. Are you likely to change from a selfish, violent young man into something a little more pleasant?"
He looked at me with a degree of anger and then his face softened a little.

"You mean why should you save somebody who's the scum of the earth?"
"I wouldn't go as far as to say that, but if I did attempt to help you, I would want to know that you didn't continue to be a thieving, drunken wife-beater!"

"You don't pull any punches do you?"
"Well, what would you call yourself? People are defined by what they say and do. Only you are in charge of what you say, what you think and what you do, nobody else. Think about it! Even if I could save you, I am not sure I would want to!"

"I suppose I can't blame you for thinking like that, but I will promise to change."
"Words are very easy to say, deeds are a little bit harder. Maybe there is one way of helping you but you have to die again first!"
"What do you mean?"
"Well, it seems as if I am stuck in some kind of time-warp, and whichever 'corridor of transit' I use I

finish up on the hill the boys use for sledging with a broken ankle and blood dripping from my nose."

"Not a good place to return to over and over again."
"No, it's painful."
"But you said that you might be able to help me if I die again, how?"
"It depends on me not getting caught by the police and being able to visit your wife."
"Why do you want to do that?"
"So that you can reassure her and me that if you do come back to life, you will treat her with the respect and dignity she deserves."

"She won't be able to hear or see me."
"You're forgetting that I can make anybody see and hear you."
"Oh yes, I forgot, but last time she fainted."
"Possibly she may do again, but she will come round just like Hester did when she first saw the ghost of her husband, Valentine."

"Did they get back together?"
"Well, yes and no. I found someone with the same powers that I have and from time to time she uses them to allow Hester and Valentine to be together. It's not a perfect arrangement but it's better than what they had before."
"You mean he stayed as a ghost and his wife had to touch somebody else in order to see him?"
"That's about it."

"I'm not sure I want that!"

Eva and the Winter of 63

"Beggars can't be choosers. Anyway I haven't met anyone in 1963 with the same powers as I have and I do not plan to stay around any longer than I have to. I have a husband and three children to get back to in 2048."

"Where do they think you are at the moment?"

"At an antique fair in Brighton, but the problem is that I didn't say that I would be staying there for six weeks."

"It's going to take some explaining when you get back."

"Yes, it is. Anyway let's get back to your problem. If you can make up your differences with your wife and promise to be a good husband, I'll see what I can do, but I cannot promise anything for certain. Did you at any time from the Wednesday before your death until the Sunday pass this hospital?"

"No, I don't think so."

"Do you know the name of the blonde that you had your fling with?"

"Why?"

"Well, if I can't alter the things you did running up to your death, I might be able to alter her behaviour."

"Good thinking Eva. Yes, her name is Julia Bromley."

"Somehow, I need to find out what she was doing on the Saturday of the weekend you died. Maybe you can watch her over the next few days and tell me what she does, particularly if she comes close to this hospital or anywhere where we can change what she does."

"But it will be too late to do that. I die on the Sunday evening."

"You're forgetting the time-warp I'm in. We cannot solve the problem this time around but maybe we can the next time!"

"You'll break your ankle again for me?"

"It seems that I have no option."

Diverting Julia Bromley

I had my visits from the boys yet again that week and of course my frustrating interview with Detective Inspectors Rosebury and Bowers. It didn't go any better this time than the first time, as I was unable to contain my annoyance at their attitude.

I was read my rights again and threatened with detention as soon as my ankle was repaired enough for me to be transferred to the town's police station. Until that time I was watched over by the same stream of young policemen.

I didn't see Graham on the day he died; in fact I didn't see him again for the rest of the next week. It wasn't until I was holed up in St James' Church after my second perfect escape from the hospital that I met up with him again.

"Why has it taken such a long time for you to get back to me?" I said as he appeared in the church.
"It has been difficult for me to work out what we can do."
"I only asked you to find out about Julia, not to come up with a plan."
"Yes, I realise that but I know Julia and Carole better than you do, so I wanted to help you devise a plan."
"You said that you just bumped into Julia at the pub on that Saturday night!"

"I'm sorry. I didn't quite tell the truth about that."
"How on earth do you expect me to help you when you tell me lies?" I was getting really angry.
"Julia had been a former girlfriend of mine before I met Carole."
"So this wasn't just a 'one night stand' situation?"
"Yes, it was. The only thing I hadn't said was that I knew Julia from before."
"Deliberately omitting something which you should have said is just the same as lying."

"OK, can I please get on with what I have found out?"
"I'm listening."
"Julia only goes to the pub on Saturday because her friend Jennifer wants her to so she can meet this boy that she's been after. Sort of like an excuse, pretending that they're there by accident, so to speak. Anyway, Julia didn't want to go to start with, because she didn't fancy being a gooseberry. That's why she was so pleased to see me."
"Even though she knew you were married?"
"I'm not sure she did."

Eva and the Winter of 63

"And you didn't tell her?"
"No, I didn't." His demeanour changed. "Look, I know I did wrong but I was angry with Carole."
"That's no excuse for what you did."
"No, it isn't."
"Go on, tell me what you found out."

"Well, this boy that Jennifer fancies is only the older brother of one of them boys that are helping you."
"Which one?"
"The oldest one. The tallest one."
"Derek?"
"Yes, Derek O'Rourke. His brother is called Michael."
"So is his Dad."
"Yes, but the son is often referred to as Mick."

"Does Jennifer succeed in 'getting off' with this Mick?"
"What do you mean 'getting off'?"
"Does her plan succeed and she becomes his girlfriend."
"Well, that's the thing, Mick doesn't go to that pub on Saturday, for some reason he went to another pub with his mates."

"What have you being doing for the last few days since Sunday?"
"I went to see Carole."
"Why?"
"Because seeing her at the funeral, I needed to know if she missed me or was she still really angry at the way I had treated her."
"And?"

"She has cried everyday since I died. She is really upset and blames herself for what happened."
"Don't you dare start thinking that. It was your fault and your fault alone!" I wasn't going to let him of the hook.
"Yes, I know."

"Anyway, what was the plan you've taken all this time to come up with?"
"It's simple really, now we know why Julia was at the pub."
"Which pub was it?"
"The Rising Sun. Do you know it?"
"Yes, it's still there in 2048 but I guess it looks a little different."
"My plan is that you give Derek a message to take to Jennifer that Mick is not going to The Rising Sun but to the Four Ways pub on Saturday. The Four Ways pub is just on the corner, not far from here. Do you know that one?"
"No, they must have knocked it down at some point, just like they knock this lovely church down."

"Anyway do you think that you can ask Derek to give Jennifer the message?"
"The difficulty is; why would I be asking Derek to tell a girl I have never met that his brother, who probably doesn't know the girl, will be in the Four Ways pub on Saturday 12th January?"
"Hmm, I see your point."
"He'll just think I'm more of a lunatic than he first imagined! We could never be sure that he would carry out what I had asked him to do. He could probably say 'yes' he would do it and not bother."

Eva and the Winter of 63

"We could scare him into doing it!"

"Just how do you think we could do that?"
"You've told me quite a few amusing stories about how you scared people when you were younger. The story of the two ghosts who could make their heads fall off because they had been beheaded sounds good to me."
"Go get me a sharp knife then!"

"Ha! Very funny, but there must be something we can do."
"Let me have a think about it. There may be a way I can disguise the request so that it makes more sense. They did take me to Bessie's funeral after all."

Funeral take two

If I was to try and help Graham, I first had to decide whether or not it was for the better. I had always tried not to alter the course of history and I certainly did not want to do it for some violent wife-beater. I needed to make sure that he was worth saving. This could only mean meeting Carole.

After much deliberation, I thought that it was better all round if at the next 'Graham and Bessie' funeral I got caught and put in prison or whatever they planned to do with me.

It would save the boys the trouble of visiting me and bringing me provisions etc. It would mean that I was somewhere warm and being fed hot meals on a regular basis.

As before, I caught the bus with Derek, John and Alan and, of course, Graham, to the cemetery at Four

Eva and the Winter of 63

Lane Ends. This time I didn't go into Graham's 'corridor of transit' when Carole fainted. I let the driver of the limousine hold on to me.

To start with, no one knew what to do with me. Anyway, there was something more of a priority to deal with first, as poor Carole was still laid on the gravel unconscious. Even in this situation I tried to be the helpful one.

"Raise her legs a little to let the blood go to her head," I said.

They ignored me. Slowly a very groggy Carole came round and sat up. She had a graze down the right-hand side of her face with droplets of blood appearing. Her tights (or were they stockings?) were laddered after the impact with the gravel.

She got to her feet with the aid of a burly woman who appeared to be taking charge of the situation. She looked at me again and then for a second time she looked over my shoulder. This time however she could not see Graham as she was no longer in contact with me.

A 'kind' man said that he would go to the caretaker's lodge and try and phone 999 for the police. Since there were no mobile phones it meant that it was either this or using the public phone box near the bus shelter where we had been dropped off.

"I saw Graham," Carole stammered, "I saw Graham stood behind this lady."

The burly woman, who presumably was her mother, tried to comfort her. "Yes dear, of course. You are very upset."
"No, I saw Graham," she repeated, "I saw him standing over there when this lady touched me. I could see him."
Naturally she was getting very emotional once again.

After a few minutes in which she stood bewildered by the events, she spoke to me.
"Who are you?"
"A Russian spy," replied her mother before I had chance to think of something sensible to say.

"Could I have a word with you Carole in private?"
"No, you can't," came the protective response from her mother, "look what you have done to her already. We need to get you to a doctor, Carole."

Physically, I had done nothing to cause her injury. OK my actions had caused her to faint.
I repeated my question. "At some time in the future I would like to talk to you. May I come and see you?"
"You'll be in prison!"
Her mother was beginning to annoy me, even though her behaviour was understandable.
"Can I come and see you?" I tried for a third time.

"Who are you?" Carole said yet again.
I had spent some time thinking about this obvious question and the best I could do had been well-rehearsed.
"I am a medium. I can speak to the dead and Graham came to me and asked if I could help him. What you saw was Graham but you can only see him when I allow it to happen."

Eva and the Winter of 63

"What rubbish! Don't listen to her, Carole. She's Russian and clearly mad."
Of course, the Russians were the current 'baddies' but I doubted that they were all mad! Over time, the country where the 'baddies' came from had changed, but there had to be 'baddies'.

"I am NOT Russian and I am NOT mad," I found myself saying angrily.
What happened next was unexpected.
"Can you show me Graham again?" Carole said.
"Are you sure?"
"Don't be silly, Carole."
"Please Mum, I believe this lady. I know what I saw."

"Look, before the police take me away, will you please promise to come and see me so we can talk?"
"Yes, of course. Please let me see Graham again. I still love him."

That remark reinforced my instincts that maybe what I was about to attempt was for the good. I walked slowly towards her and gently touched her on the arm. Graham was again stood behind me.

Although Carole's face showed shock yet again, she did not faint but stood staring over my shoulder.
"Graham," she said softly.
"Carole," came the reply, "I am really sorry for what I have done and with Eva here I have come to make amends for everything that I have done wrong."

There was a distant noise unlike anything that I had ever heard before. It was all bells and there was none of the wailing of sirens that I was used to indicating the presence of emergency vehicles. The driver who had maintained his grip on me pulled me away and Carole lost sight of her husband once again.

As I was marched towards the sirens, Carole said "I will come and see you, I promise."

Interrogations

After an hour or so spent not quite in solitary confinement, as Graham was present for most of the time, I was summoned before DI Rosebury and a gentleman from London who introduced himself as Mr Wilson. It didn't seem real somehow. My mind went back to some really old films, which probably hadn't even been done yet, involving James Bond 007. Wasn't there one film called 'From Russia With Love'? My grandparents had been really keen on these spy films with their Ms and Qs and MI5 or was it 6 or 7?

The world of 2048 did not have these quaint names. With the coming of the World Wide Web, the Global Village and satellites, there were a lot more sophisticated spying agents than men dressed in suits with pens designed to shoot bullets.

In 2048, countries found it much more difficult to hide what they were doing illegally. 'Big Brother' really had arrived one hundred years after George Orwell had written his famous book '1984'. I knew all this because I had recently seen a history programme which was celebrating the hundredth anniversary of the book.

I was brought back to the present when Mr Wilson spoke, "We have reasons to believe that you have been spying for the Russians or some other agency."
"What reasons?"
Momentarily he was a bit taken aback by my slightly aggressive response.

"Mrs Mills, we have guns and devices that belong to you and therefore these give us our reasons."
"I have told DI Rosebury what they are. Hasn't he told you?"
"Yes, he says that you say that the guns are from the First World War and the devices are something to do with computers and cameras."

"That is very accurate. Surely you have had an expert look at the guns?"
"Yes."
"And what did they say about them?"
"They appear to be from the First World War," he said quietly.
"And the camera that you mentioned is a phone that can take pictures."
"There we have a problem believing you, Mrs Mills. Yes, our experts say that the device is of a kind of technology that they have never seen before but it can certainly take pictures of high quality."

Eva and the Winter of 63

"And what's more it is made in Japan, not Russia, and do I look Japanese to you, Mr Wilson?"
"Spies are never what they appear, Mrs Mills, that's why they are spies."

"Look, what are you planning to do with me? You have no evidence of me spying, only the fact that I possess some technological devices that your experts don't understand. I have tried to explain to DI Rosebury but he isn't bright enough to understand!"

DI Rosebury bristled at this insult, whilst Mr Wilson smiled, presumably at the 'local' policeman's discomfort.
"Are you bright enough Mr Wilson?"
His smile disappeared.

"There are questions you have still to answer satisfactorily, Mrs Mills."
"Such as?"
"Such as, why can't we find any record of your existence in this country or any address of where you live?"
"Because I am not born for another thirty-two years and currently the house in which I live is a church."
It was DI Rosebury's turn to smile.

"Are you saying that you can travel through time?"
"Yes, that's right. That's the most intelligent question I have heard in weeks!"
Neither of them smiled!
"Yes, I can travel through time and when the time is right, I shall prove it to you."

They looked at each other and DI Rosebury said, "Maybe we could get Doctor Hawcutt to take a look at Mrs Mills?"
"Is he a shrink?" I asked.
They looked at me blankly.
"Is he a trick cyclist?" I was beginning to enjoy this interrogation. "OK, is he a Psychoanalyst?"

Understandably they seemed somewhat taken aback by these questions.
"He is a doctor that specialises in the state of people's minds."
With that I was escorted back to my cell.

"You did alright then Eva," Graham said when we were alone. He still whispered as if anybody else could hear him.

"I don't think that they understood, but I cannot really blame them. John had the same problem in 2006 when we came back with Valentine from the 17th century."
"What are you going to do now, Eva?"
"Well, it depends on Carole. The sooner she visits me, the sooner I can make a decision whether I am going to help you and then get back home."

"You cannot do that without my help," Graham said with a slight menace in his voice.
"There are plenty of other ghosts around that can help me," I lied.

Eva and the Winter of 63

The interview with Doctor Hawcutt would have made a wonderful comedy sketch. Essentially he was trying to assess the state of my mind. I attempted to answer all his questions as sensibly and accurately as I could. It was basically one of those word association tests and for the early part it went well and drew nods from the earnest doctor.

He said "Dog" and I said "Cat", he said "Boy", I said 'Girl', but then he said "Orange" and before I knew it I had said "Mobile phone".
He stopped, looked at me and presumably wrote down my response.
"Grass."
"Drugs."
A look of concern came over the doctor's face again.
"Apple."
"IPOD, IPAD and IDESK."

He stopped once again and looked at me. "How do you spell those last three words?" I spelled them out slowly.

I suppose I could have been a little more traditional but I was getting bored and was of the opinion that a home for those with mental problems might suit me a little more than a prison cell. I thought that I had more chance of escaping from such a home to see Carole than from a prison cell, and possibly she would be more likely to come and see me in the more relaxed surroundings of a home.

As the 'test' went on it seemed to get even more bizarre for the poor doctor, but not for me.

"Joy" was met with the perfectly reasonable "Rider."
"Road" with the word "Rage."
On each occasion the good doctor tutted and wrote something down. In my opinion they were perfectly good 'word associations' so I just smiled.

The final straw for the doctor came when he said the word "Lady".
My reply was "GaGa". She had been a singer who had been in her heyday whilst I was a teenager, so once again a very reasonable response.

He dropped his pen, scratched his head and sighed. Doctor Hawcutt was now very agitated at my 'associations' even though technically they were very accurate but just not ones he understood from his life in the 1960s.

"I think that we will end the session there," he said resignedly, "I think I have heard enough to make my decision," he muttered.

By the end of the session it was clear that my transfer to a hospital for patients with mental disorders was assured.

Royd's Hall

Whether it was a good move for me I was yet to find out, but the powers that be decided that Royd's Hall would be the best place to put me for the time being whilst they decided if I was a real danger to society.

Doctor Hawcutt had clearly advised them that I had 'mental' issues which needed further treatment and that a room at Royd's Hall would be a better place than a prison cell. I arrived with my meagre possessions at Royd's Hall on Wednesday 30th January.

The good news was that the very cold weather was beginning to abate and it was getting fairly warm with a degree of sunshine.

Royd's Hall was an old building probably built in the 1920s as a manor house for a rich family but had been taken over as a 'mental hospital' or maybe recuperation hospital after the Second World War. My room was on the top floor of the three-storey house. I assume that this was under the orders of DI Rosebury as it might be a bit more difficult to escape from there. I was to be confined to my room which was again guarded by a police officer.

I was allowed downstairs to the 'dayroom' as it was called from time to time and of course to go there to eat lunch and dinner. The 'inmates', for the want of a better name, were a varied and interesting bunch. Some patients were clearly in the grip of what I knew to be Alzheimer's disease, a name, I began to realize, that wasn't used by the staff. Sadly I had had an aunt who suffered from the disease and I recognised the bewildered look on their faces as their visitors arrived and they hadn't a clue who they were. It was better in 2048 because they had discovered a drug which slowed down the degenerative process of the disease and which meant people lived longer with an increased quality of life.

They were all, in their own way, interested in me being there. I was, with one exception, the youngest there.

The exception was a young girl, maybe in her early to mid twenties, who twisted her hair frequently in a nervous behaviour. This signalled her out as not being one of the 'carers' who were in the main a little bit older. Her name was Brenda and she was slim with jet black hair and black-rimmed glasses.

I made a point of smiling at her each time we met and more often than not she smiled back. She had a number of visitors, possibly her parents and her sisters and they fussed over her on every visit.

I had not told the boys where I was and I hoped that the authorities hadn't done so. So when visiting times came around I was able to observe the visitors and how the people they visited behaved. The thing about Brenda was that in the dayroom she had been quite talkative and almost, one might say, extrovert in her behaviour. When her visitors arrived she didn't say a word and virtually shunned them.

After the Friday afternoon visiting time had ended, I asked my 'guardian' angel, a young PC called Trevor, if I could remain in the dayroom. I guess he preferred being downstairs to outside my room on the third floor. Downstairs, he could talk to the young blonde carer and since I was an expert on the topic, their body language told me that they quite fancied each other.

I waited for Brenda to return to the dayroom after saying the silent 'good-bye' to her visitors. I got up from my position near the window to join her at the table where she had joined two other ladies.
"Hi Brenda. Are you alright?"
"No! I hate visiting time. They never believe anything I have to say and just patronise me," she twisted her hair in anger.
"What don't they believe?"
She looked at me as if to say, 'It's nothing to do with you'.

"I might be able to help you if you let me." I was taking a risk but felt that there was something about her I recognised.

She hesitated and then whispered, "Can we talk in private?"

We returned to the seats in the window that I had left a few moments earlier. Once seated, she whispered to me again. "Do you believe in ghosts?"

I knew it! That's what I recognised in her, as I had done with Lucy in 1605. She saw ghosts and nobody believed her but unlike Lucy she was not under the threat of being burnt at the stake. However to be locked away in an institution for what she could see seemed just as horrific and I was pleased that I had been born in 1995 not in the 1930s or 40s as she had.

"Yes," I whispered back. She smiled and looked pleased at my response.

"Have you seen ghosts in here as well?"

"No I haven't, but I have seen them at other places." This was the truth as I had seen no other ghost apart from Graham since the bombs went off in 1916. It was still worrying me that my powers appeared to be much reduced.

"There is a ghost of a lady who walks along on my landing. I have seen her many times."

"How long have you been able to see ghosts from the spirit world?"

"The first thing that I can remember was when I was about nine. An old man haunted the school I went to

Eva and the Winter of 63

and I saw him in the playground. Nobody believed me as nobody else could see him. They thought I was just telling silly stories and exaggerating things but I knew I wasn't."
"What happened?"
"Well, to start with they just thought of me as someone who lied but then my parents decided that I be 'looked at' and the doctors diagnosed me as 'mad', but I am not 'mad'. I do see what I say I see."

"I believe you. The doctors have decided that I am mad for the same reasons."
"But they said that you were a crazy and dangerous Russian spy and they are just keeping you here until they work out what to do with you."

"Rumours tend to exaggerate things. Would you believe me if I said that I too could see ghosts and have been able to for many years?"
"You can?"
"Yes and what's more I can use them to travel back in time and that's what has led to the rumour that I am a spy."
"How do you do that? Can you show me how?"
"Can we take this one step at a time? We don't want to scare anybody."

"Do you want to meet my ghost?"
"Yes, would you like to meet the gentleman I have met?"
"But you said that you hadn't met a ghost here!"
"I haven't yet but I met a man in a church when the police were after me."

"That's wonderful that you believe me and have had some of the same experiences. It makes me so sad and angry that nobody will believe me. Let's go see if Melba is around."

At that we got up and left the dayroom.

Meeting Melba

We took the stairs to the second floor where her room was situated. Trevor followed.
"Can we get rid of that policeman?" Brenda whispered.
"I doubt it, although there might be a way."

"She is usually around here somewhere. Ah there she is, near the window at the end of the corridor."

I couldn't see her!
"Where did you say she was?"
"At the window, can't you see her?"
"Oh yes, I can see her now," I lied.

I couldn't see anything! I was screaming inside!
Why can't I see her? What has happened to me? It must have been that bomb in 1916. It's done something to me and my powers!

I tried to compose myself and did the only thing I could think of that would help, I took hold of Brenda's hand. Melba appeared as I thought she would. She was a bit like my Eva, my first apparition, slim and dressed in 1920s clothes as if she was off to a dance. She smiled as we approached hand in hand, then her face went from a beautiful smile to a frown.

I realized that Trevor dressed in his policeman's uniform was the reason for her consternation. I thought that I might 'kill two birds with one stone'.
"Come here Trevor and meet Melba."
He looked puzzled, so I walked away from Brenda, took the somewhat surprised Trevor by the hand and returned to where Brenda was standing and once again held her hand. He went pale.

"What's wrong Trevor, you look as if you've seen a ghost!"
"I . . . I don't feel well. Who is that?"
"That's Melba. And you are right she is a ghost."
"There's no such thing. It's one of your spying tricks," and he broke away and went back downstairs in something of a hurry.

"That's the reaction I usually get when people see me!" said Melba. "Good afternoon Brenda and who is this woman who is not scared at seeing me?"

"This is my friend Eva, she's a Russian spy!"
"No I am not," I retorted, somewhat hurt by the remark, "I am someone who has the powers to be able to see people who have died and travel in time through their 'corridors of transit'."

Eva and the Winter of 63

Well at least I could do that until my little mishap!

"You can?" said Melba.
"You can do what?" said Brenda.
"Can I show her, Melba?"
"Yes of course."
"But where will we go?"
"You have a choice. I died in this house but was born in Matlock in Derbyshire."
"When were you born?"
"1887."
"And when did you die?"
"1940."
"Can we take the 1940 option please?"
"What on earth are you two talking about?"
"Wait and see, all will be explained. Keep hold of my hand and walk towards Melba."

The familiar bright lights and tunnel were soon surrounding us, well familiar that is to me. Poor Brenda looked a little nervous.
Soon we were in the same corridor where we had started.

"Nothing has happened," said Brenda.
"Oh yes it has!"
There were voices coming from downstairs. "Melba's fallen; I think that she might be dead! Quick, get the doctor!"

There before us was a prone Melba and there at the side of her body was the ghostly version of the same woman.

"Quick, get into that room."
I pulled a bewildered Brenda into the room Melba had indicated and closed the door.

"What's going on? I don't understand," she said.
"Shush. They'll hear you."
"Who will?"
"Let me explain what has happened," I whispered, "we are still in Royd's Hall and on the second floor but it's the year 1940. I am not sure what date it is because it's the day Melba died."
"I still don't understand. This is not my room. Look at all the strange ornaments, although the curtains, the carpets and even the wallpaper are the same."

"I don't know whether this is your room or not but as I said the year is 1940!"
"Why 1940?"
"Didn't you hear Melba say that she had died in 1940? Didn't you notice that there were two Melbas out there? There was the dead one on the floor where she had presumably just fallen and the . . ." I hesitated because I was just about to say 'live' one, "and the ghost one who spoke to us!"

"How do you know that the one on the floor was Melba? I couldn't see her face."
"Well, one of the 'corridors of transit' of all ghosts leads them to the place and time of their death. On my request Melba chose that one for us to walk down. If it had been the time and place of her birth we would have seen her as a baby."

Eva and the Winter of 63

"I think I see what you mean. I have a lot to learn haven't I?"

"Yes, but it will come to you in time. Our main problem at the moment is that we need to get out of the house before we are discovered hiding in this room. The best place to go would be those gardens out there and then we can wait until things settle down a bit. With Melba dying there'll be quite a lot of activity on the landing for a time."

"You've still to explain again exactly what ha. happened to us."

"When we've got away from the house, I'll explain as best I can, but it is complicated."

I could still hear voices outside the door. Mild pandemonium was taking place at the tragedy that had just occurred.

"We need to wait here quietly until all the fuss has died down."

"You say that we are in Royd's Hall but the year has changed." Brenda was still wrestling with the enormity of what had just happened to her and probably the consequences of the powers she had.

"Yes, so you won't recognize the people who are out there and what's more they won't recognize either you or me. They may think that we had something to do with Melba's death."

"How did she die?"

"I guess that she had a nasty fall but it could have been a heart attack. I'll ask her later."

"Strange asking somebody how they died, isn't it?"
"Yes, but it is part of the power we've been given and there are even stranger things as you will discover."

We waited until the noise had died down completely and presumably they had taken poor Melba's body downstairs.

Whilst we were waiting in the room, I again heard that strange ringing of bells that I had heard in the cemetery, as the ambulance arrived.

"Remember that it's 1940 Brenda, so be careful what you say should anybody want to speak to us. I don't want to be locked away in 1940 as well as 1963!
"So you are not a Russian spy. This is what has happened to you before isn't it?"
"I am no more a Russian spy than you are mad. Yes, I came from the future down somebody's 'corridor of transit' just like we did with Melba, and into 1916 to collect some antique guns. Something drastic must have happened after a bomb went off and somehow I got stuck in 1963."

"How are you going to get home?"
"I'm hoping that maybe Melba can help me. You said that I'm not a Russian spy but by the same token you're not mad and we need to convince other people of this and get you out of Royd's Hall to live a normal, well nearly normal life."

Eva and the Winter of 63

"No, you are right, I am not mad but I cannot convince other people of that."

"I can help, I think."
"Why are you not sure?"
"Well, I haven't been entirely honest with you. I did have the same powers as you, but I appear to have lost some of them. I couldn't see Melba to start with. Only when I held your hand could I see her and it was your power that I was using, not mine. It's a power you have in that if you touch someone, they can see the same things as you can."

"I've got the power to do that?"
"Yes, I found out by accident that I could do that and it has scared a few people, sometimes for the better! Be careful though, it can be very dangerous and get you into a lot of trouble as I have recently found out. That poor policeman Trevor will find it hard to explain to his seniors why he has lost me. Gone without a trace!"

"This sounds like fun!"

We cautiously left the room. There was no sign of anyone on the landing where Melba had died. As we went down the stairs, rather slowly since the pot on my leg still hampered my mobility, I could see a lot of people milling about in the entrance hall.

I was worried that the way we were dressed would single us out for attention. Fortunately the people appeared more engrossed in conversation about what had just happened to Melba, to notice two strangers coming down the stairs and exiting via the main door.

Once out in the garden, I felt better. It was clearly summer and the sun shone brightly. We walked down the large drive which led from the house. Brenda may not have noticed the people in the entrance hall and the way they were dressed, but she couldn't fail to notice all the soldiers and armed vehicles that surrounded the house. They must have been trying to convert the house into a military hospital or headquarters.

"What are all these soldiers doing at the house?"
"It's 1940. The Second World War has just started. Weren't there a lot of soldiers killed and injured on the beaches of France?"
"Oh yes, at Dunkirk. I don't remember it that well as it happened in the year I was born, but I do remember learning a bit about it at school. A lot of men lost their lives on the beaches at Dunkirk. It was terrible. Maybe a lot of badly injured soldiers are in make-shift hospitals in the south and they have brought those with lesser injuries up to Yorkshire."
"Possibly."
"Why is it so sunny? Where has all the snow gone?"
"Melba must have died in the summer. It must be June or July."
"What are we going to do now?"
"I really need to get back to 1963. I have some important things to do."
"Such as?"

Eva and the Winter of 63

I explained about Graham and what I was going to try and do if I thought that it was wise to bring him back to life.

"Can we do those sorts of things?"
"I'm not sure Brenda, and I am really not sure I want to."
"Why bring injured soldiers all the way up here?"
"Many large mansion houses were commandeered during the war as hospitals. The normal hospitals just couldn't cope with all the casualties of the war.

Several soldiers approached us, each having some bandages on various parts of their bodies, eyes, arms and heads.
"Good afternoon," they said as they passed by.
"Could I stay here and look after them?" asked Brenda.
"You could but remember that at some time there will be another younger Brenda arriving at some time. When did they send you here?"
"1954."
"So you were fourteen, a troublesome teenager?"

Before she could reply to the accusation, we were interrupted.
"Excuse me, but do you know where Major Collingwood can be found?" It was a soldier with an eye patch who had clearly just arrived.
"Sorry, we are new here too, but there were some officers in the entrance hall that might know." I tried to be helpful. He left towards the house.

"It looks like this is the beginning of the change from a mansion house to a military hospital."

"That means Melba used to live in this posh house. She must be a real Lady, maybe even a Countess."
"I doubt it," I said, "but certainly she must have come from a rich family."

We watched as many soldiers arrived in various military vehicles and made their way up to the house.
"What are we going to do?" Brenda asked again.
"Find Melba and go back to 1963."
"Can I come back here at any time?"
"Yes, but it will always be 1940. But be careful, the longer you stay here the more you'll be missed at Royd's Hall in 1963."

"I don't care about that! Here I can have a normal life with people who don't think that I'm mad."
"Perhaps the best compromise is to come back here from time to time with Melba's help? Maybe you ought to build bridges with your family and stop talking about seeing ghosts and become a good nurse! My advice is to keep the spiritual side of your life as secret as you can."

"Eva, I love you. You have given me hope and something to live for and maybe I can now lead a normal life outside a mental hospital!"

Returning from the War

There were literally hundreds of soldiers around the gardens. It was difficult to see how the home would cope with so many. I needed to find Melba and return to 1963 as soon as possible.

Although the pot on my leg hindered my mobility, I was now getting around much better. I assumed that the same 'pot technology' was available in 1940 as it was in 1963. However, I was beginning to have a problem with Brenda. Simply put, she didn't want to return to 1963. She thought that she would be really happy being a nurse to wounded soldiers.

In truth, I too believed that she would make a really caring nurse. However, I could not get back without her. I couldn't see Melba without her help and so the transfer to 1963 was impossible to do myself. This was really frustrating for me.

In the end, after much discussion, she agreed to take me back if we could stay here for the day. Following that, she said that she would return immediately to 1940. However, her help came at a price. I had to promise to try and cover for her at Royd's Hall back in 1963. That promise was not going to be easy to keep, but I vowed that I would try my best.

Nobody really questioned us as we went back into the hall and not even as we walked around some of the downstairs rooms. Probably that was because everybody was new and in the confusion of people arriving, two more 'new' people were not going to be noticed, provided we blended in.

Brenda was really keen to be of help and without telling me she approached an elderly lady who seemed to be in charge of meeting people as they arrived.

"I'm a nurse and have been sent to help," I heard Brenda say to the woman.
"What's your name?"
"Brenda Douglas."
"You're not on my list."
"I should be," Brenda said with some conviction.
"Things are a bit chaotic at the moment. Go into that room and ask for Matron. She will get you a uniform and tell you what your duties are."

"What have you done?" I asked her as she returned to me.
"I've got a job!"
"You can't stay here for ever."

Eva and the Winter of 63

"Why not?"
"Because in 1954 another, much younger, Brenda is going to arrive as a patient!"
"Maybe I can help her because I remember being so unhappy when I arrived."

"You are dabbling with things that neither of us understand."
"I prefer a life here as a nurse than back there as a patient."
"What about your family?"
"Don't care about them. They haven't been all that nice to me."
"OK. We are getting nowhere."

"I have to go into that room over there to get my uniform."
"Are you really, really sure about this?"
"I have never been so sure about anything in my life!"
"I won't be able to cover for you for ever. I want to get home once I have sorted Graham's problem and of course solved mine."
"No problem Eva. You've been a good friend to me and you have given me a life that I never thought I would have."
"Please take me back."
"Once I've collected my uniform and have been told what my duties are, I promise to take you back," and with that she walked away.

Another group of soldiers entered the hall and walked towards me.
"Excuse me lady," one of them said. "Do we report to you? We've only just arrived."

They were four very young-looking men, hardly out of their teens and yet they had been through so much.
"We're Royal Engineers from the Third Army. Jack, Henry and me, we're from Eastbourne, and Harry here is from Lewes."

"You've got the wrong person. That lady over there is the one you want."
"I do hope that your leg gets better. Was it shrapnel?" Harry asked.
"No, nothing as dangerous as that," I didn't elaborate.
The four walked away and Harry looked back and gave me a smile that I thought I recognized. His eyes somehow seemed so familiar.

At that moment Brenda arrived back, dressed in a nurse's uniform.
"Come with me dear," she said with a smile.
'Dear' indeed! Suddenly she was a different person and playing a role that she appeared to enjoy.

I dutifully followed her, limping along behind her and slowly climbed the stairs. We walked into a number of rooms where Brenda assumed the responsibility of tending to the injured soldiers. She comforted them; made repairs to their bandages; carried and fetched at their request. This went on for a couple of hours and I couldn't be anything but impressed by her demeanour and skills in the job she had just usurped with no training or education.

Eventually, I took her to one side and I tried to warn her. "You are a lovely person Brenda, but please be

Eva and the Winter of 63

carful. Remember you cannot mention anything that has happened in the twenty-three years from 1940 to 1963 and that includes who won the war."

She smiled sweetly and replied, "I understand. I am not as stupid or mad as people think, you know."
"I know that, Brenda," I said, realising that I had just been slightly reprimanded.

We walked, or in my case hobbled, to the landing where we had appeared some hours earlier.
"She's over there in the usual place," Brenda said as we arrived, "I think she must have been waiting for us to return."

"Hi Melba!" she called out, slightly too loudly for my liking.
I still couldn't see anything remotely like a ghost on the empty landing but continued the theme.
"Hi Melba!"

"Hand please Eva," came her command as if she was a nurse asking a patient.
"Remember you have no training as a nurse."
"Yes, I have! I've watched nurses for the last nine years. I know how to care for people."
With that, we once again walked hand in hand towards Melba.

In one way we were unlucky because there were two ladies on the landing as we arrived. They were really shocked at our sudden appearance and both screamed.

"I'll deal with them, you stay here," suggested Brenda.
"Sorry about that, Mrs Jones. Are you and Mrs Terry OK?"
"Where oh where did you come from?"
"Sorry, we just came out of my room very quickly because we thought we saw a mouse."

It was clear that Mrs Jones and Mrs Terry were confused and Brenda was clearly playing on that fact.
"Let's go and get a nice cup of tea, shall we? I really need one after seeing that mouse. I'll go and get Matron to see what she has to say."

The bemused ladies willingly followed Brenda downstairs.

I stood there alone, well not quite but to anyone else except Brenda, I was on my own. I waited for some ten minutes or so before Brenda returned. I don't quite know why I continued to wait there on the landing, maybe just to wish her well I suppose.

"Is there anything you want me to say to your parents?"
"Yes, tell them I love them but I don't like their attitude towards me and that I have gone away to start a new life."
However, before I had chance to reply, she disappeared.

I decided to return to my room, but as I was about to do so, PC Evans appeared.
"Where have you been? PC Chamberlain says you gave him the slip and disappeared."

Eva and the Winter of 63

Trevor had obviously given him a reasonable scenario for my disappearance, rather than a truthful one.
"I've been with Brenda talking about the War," not an untrue statement!

He looked at me and puffed his cheeks out in mock disbelief. He sighed and his ample stomach swelled out.
"I don't believe you."
"Well, go find Brenda and ask her."
"I will!"
"No you won't!" I mouthed.

He looked back at me, as presumably he went to find Brenda.
I felt sorry for Trevor, the young PC, as we had put him in a difficult position. I hoped that it wouldn't have too much of an effect on his career.

It was eerie to think that I had been stood inches away from a ghost and had not been able to see her. I made my way upstairs to my room and there was yet another policeman sat outside my room.
"Good evening, Mrs Mills."
I entered my room both sad and happy at what Brenda had done.

The Visit of Carole Newton

My attention turned to getting my plaster pot removed. The six week date for its removal was almost up. By my reckoning it was 13th February. There had been a bit of concern at the disappearance of Brenda and several agencies had been contacted to try and search for her as a missing person. I did what I promised her and had spoken to her parents. As far as other people were concerned, all I knew was that she had said that she was leaving to start a new life somewhere, I knew not where.

I had a surprise visit from Graham on the Thursday evening, prior to my hospital visit, just after tea had been served. Basically, he was still only interested in whether I was going to help him and bring him back to life.

"It all depends on Carole," I said to him when we were out of earshot of all the others. "I am rather

disappointed that she hasn't been to see me, so I will need to go see her."
"Why?"
"I've told you before, I am not going to help a wife-beater to come back to life. I need to talk to her to get her opinion on the situation."

His demeanour changed as he realized that I meant everything that I had said.

"I'm not a wife-beater. I just made one mistake. Did something I admit was very stupid and wrong but I repeat I'm no wife-beater."
"You did pay a high price for your dreadful mistake."
"Yes, I did."
"My first job is to escape from here for a time and go to visit Carole."

As it happened it wasn't necessary, as on Saturday afternoon Carole arrived at Royd's Hall.

My first impressions are usually quite accurate, although occasionally I get it wrong as I did with Thomas Percy in 1605.

My first impression of Carole was that she was sweet and without an aggressive bone in her body. Her demeanour was polite and friendly towards me, despite the fact that I had caused her some distress at the funeral.

"Hello, Mrs Mills. It's nice to see you again," she said with a genuine air of friendship. "How are you?"
"OK, I guess. This pot will be off my leg soon and then I can get around a bit better."

With the formalities over, I decided to go straight to the point. The problem was that at present I was not sure that I could actually reunite Graham with Carole, and didn't want to give her false hope. My reason for meeting her was to make a female assessment of the relationship between Carole and Graham. Thereafter I would make a decision regarding whether I wanted to alter history in a way I had never done before.

Yes, I had had an effect on lots of people's lives; Hester Walton, Rebecca and her children, Anne Stow and of course Grace Collin. Regarding Hester, Rebecca and Anne I felt that I had had a positive effect on their lives but I had altered Grace's life for ever and felt ashamed of what I had done to her, although her own foolishness in loving Thomas Percy in 1605 had contributed to her disfigurement.

To alter things so that a person does not die had ramifications beyond my experience. If I could do it for Graham I could do it for anyone. It would give me an almost 'God-like' power over life and death. This worried me intensely but as I sat there looking at this pretty young woman and her beehive hairstyle, I couldn't help but feel positive towards her and the unborn baby that she was carrying.

"Are you alright?" I asked.

Eva and the Winter of 63

"Yes, just about. Sorry I haven't been sooner what with the funeral and the baby . . . ."
"Yes, I understand. Is the baby ok?"
"From the way he or she has been kicking, I would say so."
In 2048 she would probably have known which sex the baby was, although it was still an option for mothers-to-be not to know.

"At the funeral you said that you wanted to talk to me about something. Do you remember Mrs Mills?"
"Call me Eva, please Carole. Yes, I do need to talk to you, but I'm not sure how I can put this."
"Put what?"
"Well, here goes, I have these special powers that let me see both the living and the dead and, as you found out at the funeral, anyone who touches me can temporarily share these powers."

"You mean I could see and talk to Graham again?"
"Yes."
"Is he here now?"
"No, but he was yesterday. I could ask him next time. I'm sure that he would want to meet you again."
"I'm free most days and I can get the bus here quite easily."
"How about tomorrow afternoon? I'm bound to see him before then."
"Yes, that would be super."
"I'll ask the policeman on duty if we could meet in my room."
"Policeman?"

"Yes, since the funeral I have been under police surveillance as a suspected Russian spy."
"Oh yes, I'm sorry about what my mother said and the trouble you got into at the funeral."
"It's OK."

We proceeded to chat about all manner of things; mainly about the baby and my own three children; how she felt about being a mother; and of course the awful weather and how it was getting warmer. We British have always talked about one of the most unpredictable influences on our lives.

She was simply a very nice person caught up in an unfortunate series of events that had had a devastating effect on her life and that of her unborn baby.

We parted just as amicably as we had met and she promised to return on the Sunday afternoon.

Graham arrived early that evening as if he knew that Carole had been to see me.
"Are you available to come and talk to Carole tomorrow afternoon?" I enquired. "She has agreed to meet you then."
"Yes, of course. What shall I say to her?"
"Sorry would be a good start! I would like to leave you alone to talk but sadly Carole needs me so that she can see you and is able to talk to you and hear your replies. I will try my best to keep quiet although it won't be easy."

Eva and the Winter of 63

"OK. It's a deal. You keeping quiet that is!"
"I'm not sure what time she's coming, but if you're around all afternoon?"
"Yes, I'll be here. I've nothing better to do," he said with a tinge of sadness in his voice.
"Did you know she'd been this afternoon?"
"Yes," he said with a smile, "I've been watching her quite a bit."
"That's not fair. Technically she is a free woman now."
"She spends a lot of time crying so that's a good sign isn't it?"
"Depends what she's crying about!" I said with a degree of sarcasm, "she is expecting a baby with the prospect of having no husband to help her."

"I see what you mean but I believe that she really misses me."
I left it at that.

The day of Carole's visit arrived and in the morning I approached the policeman guarding me to try and gain his permission for her to see me in my room. It was the poor unfortunate Trevor again and at first he seemed a little reluctant, given the trouble that I had caused him before. I spun him a line about Carole being a dear friend who had lost her husband recently in a car accident. To add a bit of credence to my story, I gave him details of where and when the accident had happened.

Very reluctantly he gave in on the condition that I stayed in my room and didn't try to escape out of the window!

"Don't you go disappearing again like last time. You got me into a cart-load of trouble."

"Sorry again about that, but we are on the top floor and I do have this," I said pointing to my pot leg.

"You had that last time you disappeared and it didn't stop you then!"

Carole arrived at about 2.30. I met her in the dayroom and we walked, or once again in my case, hobbled to the third floor. No lift or moving staircase had been installed in 1963 although I am sure that it would have been there in 2048 if the building still existed. It would be an absolute essential to help the elderly and infirm get to their rooms.

I introduced Carole to Trevor and he had the decency to say how sorry he was for her loss. I never did tell him that her husband Graham was killed in a police car chase where he was the one being chased!

We sat facing each other in my room and awaited Graham's arrival. It had slowly dawned on me that the reason I could see Graham was that he was, for the time being, in Limbo, whereas Melba had been dead for quite a long time and had been assigned her 'corridors of transit'. At least that was my speculation and it did make some sense.

After ten minutes or so Graham arrived.

Eva and the Winter of 63

I moved so that I was now sat at the side of Carole. From this position I was able to place my hand on her arm so that she could see Graham.

She gave a slight intake of breath at her first sight of him. He was after all, in the same state as he had died and some bruises to his face had discoloured it.

"Hi!" Graham said tentatively.
"Hello," came the reply.
Graham apologised for what he had done and so did Carole who, to me, was blameless. I was definitely on Carole's side; a woman solidarity thing, I guess. Graham had, in my opinion, to grovel for what he had done. She was incredibly accepting of his apology and there were no recriminations.

If anybody had walked into the room and been able to see us and listen to the conversation, I am sure that they would have agreed that they were a loving couple.

After half an hour or so I had to interrupt, "I'll have to go soon otherwise they'll think I've disappeared again and they may come looking for me and you might get into trouble Carole."

After Carole had left, Graham became animated.
"Are we going to do it then?"
"Do what?"
"Bring me back to life!"

"Yes, we can give it a go but I can't promise anything. My powers at the moment are not what they were."
"I think they're great. You are now stuck in 1963 for a reason and that reason is me!"
"Thanks a bunch!"
"When shall we do it?"
"Now I suppose. Poor Trevor is going to have a lot more explaining to do after this disappearance."

And with that I walked towards Graham and the bright light.

Déjà vu again!

The droplets of blood fell onto the frozen snow. They fell at regular intervals and as they hit the hard frozen surface they threw out a red ring of smaller droplets, much like the effect of a firework in the sky.

I wiped my hand across my face. Yes, once again, it was my blood dripping as regularly as the beats of a metronome.

How I got in this position, on all fours staring at the ever-increasing pool of blood, was not quite a mystery to me. I was stuck in a time warp of my own making.

As expected, my thoughts were interrupted by the appearance of the two boys who I knew to be Alan and Derek.
"We are ever so sorry missus," said Derek
"You suddenly just appeared from nowhere and we couldn't get out of your way!" said Alan

As I knew it would, my left ankle was throbbing. I tried to stand but it was too painful. Once again staying on all fours was the best position for me, despite the continual loss of blood from my nose.

Alan again offered me a handkerchief which I took. I didn't need to ask where I was or what date it was, I already knew. I was once again at the bottom of 'Sledgers' Hill' in Ferry Fryston and it was New Years Day in 1963.

"I'll go and get my father. You don't look as if you can walk very far. I only live on Elmete Drive which isn't far. Just a minute," and off he ran, leaving me once again with Alan to make polite conversation.
"What's your name?" I asked.
"Alan."
"And your friend?"
"He's called Derek."
"Do you live close by?"
"Yes, on St Andrew's Road, just down there."

I knew all the answers before Alan spoke but I was trying to keep it as original as possible just in case I messed something else up.

"I think that this is the bag you were carrying when we hit you."
He picked it up and placed it a little closer to where I was now sitting. As he did so, and for a third time, the bag toppled sideways and a gun fell out.

The look on Alan's face was all too familiar. He looked understandably shocked.

Eva and the Winter of 63

When Derek returned with his father, we introduced each other and Derek duly received his fatherly ticking off, which once again he felt aggrieved about, and despite backing from Alan,
Michael O'Rourke looked disbelievingly at the two boys.

"She's got a gun!" Alan bent down and picked up the one that had fallen out of my bag and was half-hidden in the snow. This revelation was the source of all my problems but I had to follow the same route to meet Graham once again at St James' Mission.

What was to follow was all too familiar; meeting Sheila, John and PC Evans, spending the night in John's shed; my fire-lighting adventure with John's mother, Pearl, and eventually arriving in hospital at Hightown to have the 'pot' put on my leg.

The interview with the two gentlemen from the 'spy' squad didn't go any better the third time around. Maybe I was a touch more blasé and sarcastic, but my answers were roughly the same.

The escape from the hospital went as well as it had done the previous twice, except that the nerves that I had had the first time were not present and I was a bit slicker in getting into Alan's mother's clothes.

We waited for the Leeds bus to arrive at exactly the same time as before and we were soon in the relatively safe haven of Eva's and Tom's house in Three Lane Ends.

It was at this point that I had to attempt to change the course of events. Tomorrow, Sunday 13th January was the day Graham was due to be killed in the car accident.

When I thought that the time was right to put my plan into action I said, "Could you do me a small favour, please, Derek?"

It was going to be difficult to phrase.
"Yes, of course," replied Derek with an air of confidence.
"I have a friend who has a teenage daughter and, how can I put this, she has a bit of a crush on your brother, Mike."
"How do you know Mike?"
"I don't really. It's just that my friend says that her daughter knows him and likes him a lot."
Derek looked a bit concerned. "You want me to be a sort of matchmaker, do you? The problem is that I think Mike already has a girlfriend."

This was a bit of a blow.
"I thought that you wanted to help me and this would really help." I had to be determined.
"How?" asked John.
"Well," I was struggling for sensible things to say, "Bessie has been a dear friend for years and her daughter is so nice that I thought Derek's brother might just think that too."

This was as good as it was going to get.

"All I am asking you to do is to go and tell Bessie's daughter that Mike will be in the Four Ways pub tonight."

Eva and the Winter of 63

"I don't know this girl and she would think it strange for me to say that."
"OK, but she has a friend who you could tell. Her name is Julia Bromley and she knows me." That was a lie; we had never met at this point in time!

"Where does she live?" asked John resignedly, "if it means so much to you, I'll go and tell her. Do you have her address?"

It seemed silly now but I hadn't thought this through. I didn't have either girl's address, in fact I didn't even know my pretend 'Bessie' friend's daughter's name! How stupid of me!
"We could look up Julia Bromley in the telephone directory," said Alan helpfully.
"Or dial 181 181," I added.

The boys looked at me in surprise.
"181 181. What's that?" asked Derek.
"I'm getting a bit muddled, isn't there a number you can dial to get someone's telephone number?"
"It's called Directory Enquiries, but I am not sure of its number," said John.
"But you need an address first don't you?" Derek added.
"OK, not to worry. Give me a moment to come up with something."

The boys went outside to clear away the snow to allow me to go to the outside toilet without my tracks being seen. This gave me some time to think.

I had been a complete and utter fool not to think of how they could contact the girls so as to divert them from going to the Rising Sun. A simple answer then dawned on my muddled mind.

I opened the door and shouted, "I have an idea John."
John came around the corner with a puzzled look on his face. "An idea to do what?"
"See the girls and tell them Mike is in the Four Ways pub."
He still looked puzzled.

"The Rising Sun is not far away from here. You could wait 'til the girls turn up and tell them."
"I'm not old enough to go into pubs, Eva."
"You could wait outside."
"But I must get home before my parents wonder where I am."
"Could Derek do it? He's older and is after all Mike's brother."

I was being altogether too irrational and incoherent, but I was now desperate.
"I'll go ask Derek what he thinks."
I wasn't sure what was said between the boys but suddenly Derek came to the door. "I'll try and see the girls but I can't promise anything. What do they look like?"
"Julia is a very pretty girl with a blonde beehive hairdo."
"So are half the girls in the town, but I can ask around and get the right blonde."
"You must promise me that you will do it Derek. It is very important."
He seemed mystified at my insistence.

"Yes, I'll do it," and with that he rejoined the other two boys in their snow-clearing duties.

After their job was done they said their goodbyes and left. I settled down for what I knew was going to be a sleepless night and I really didn't know what I was letting myself in for by helping Graham in this way.

My major objective should have been to get my pot off and get off home. I was obviously struggling with the idea of this endless time-warp.

What I couldn't fathom out was that if Graham didn't die I would never meet him again and would lose what I regarded as my only potential 'corridor of transit' back to 2048. Was I 'cutting my nose off to spite my face' as the saying goes? Only time would tell.

Once again, I found myself requesting the presence of a ghost as I settled down for another cold, sleepless night. But sadly none came.

Escaping a time-warp

In the morning I at least remembered this time around what John had said and used hot water from the kettle to wash myself. I was now quite proficient in making tea the 'do-it-yourself' method.

John popped in as expected on his way to visit his 'colour-blind' friend Brian and I suppose to gain another undeserved victory at snooker and do a bit of homework.

Once again, he lit a fire for me with the greatest of ease.
"John?" I asked with some apprehension, "did Derek see the girls last night?"
"I don't know, I haven't seen him today."

To be brutally honest, I didn't care whether Derek had succeeded in his mission. Provided I did not go into St James' Church I would never find out whether or not Graham lived or died and in a way that was best.

Tampering with life and death did not appeal to me, so I preferred not to know whether I had the powers to do it or not.

"I would prefer to stay in the house for a few more days if you don't mind rather than go anywhere else. Is that OK with you, John?"
"Well, we thought that St James' Church would be a safer place except when they have services that is."
"I like it in this house and it would be colder in the church and harder to sleep. I assume that the church has hard benches for people to sit on."
"Yes, it has. The only problem with staying here is that my Mum and Dad might call in to check that the house is not suffering from any leaking pipes because of the freezing cold weather."

"You could ring me on your mobile if they were due to arrive."
"Sorry, I could do what?"
"Oh, never mind," I said, realizing my mistake. "I'll keep a look out and try and hide, and although your Mother will be surprised to see me she's not the kind of person to report me to the police."
"Yes, that's true."
"I'm thinking of turning myself in soon anyway."
"Why?"
"Well, they are going to catch me when I have this pot removed at the hospital so it's only a question of time. I need to get this spying matter resolved one way or another."
"You are definitely not a Russian spy!"

"Well spies don't look like spies do they, else they wouldn't be very good spies would they?"

"No, I suppose not," he agreed, "I'll get off to Brian's house. He'll wonder where I've got to. See you later in the week. Try and keep warm with the hot water bottle."

"Bye."

I had already decided to give myself up on Monday 28th January as this was the date that Graham's funeral had been and of course would be again if he was dead. If I gave myself up on this date then everything else would fall into place as it had done the last time.

The time-warp I was stuck in was a problem that I had to overcome. I spent the next few days contemplating all manner of actions which might get me home.

Occasionally, I would watch one of the two channels available on the television, BBC or ITV. How people of 1963 coped with only having two options to watch was beyond me and there was no remote and the programmes were in 2D and in black and white! My husband would have hated that. He would have had to get out of his chair and press a button on the TV! We had thousands of channels to watch, all in 3D and without those silly glasses we had to wear when I was a teenager. Without a remote how could any self-respecting man watch two films at once! My husband David used to regularly flick from channel to channel without me realizing I was watching two completely different films. They had recently brought out a TV on which you could change the channel by 'remote thinking', you just thought of the number of the

Eva and the Winter of 63

channel you wanted to watch and hey presto there it was. It was proving not to be such a great hit with large families who only had four televisions or screens, but it was progress. My own personal television was programmed to split the screen showing my favourite sixteen channels. I couldn't watch all of them at the same time of course, although my husband David claimed that he could.

Occasionally, I would catch the news which had a picture of me and the 'wanted, dangerous Russian spy' story. To start with I was angry but now I just laughed at such a ridiculous claim.

Brenda was the key to my successful return to 2048, but I had to play it differently from the last time. She had my powers and therefore with me seemingly losing some of mine, she and maybe Melba, were now the only way I could return home.

But what plan should I adopt? Should I inform Brenda as I had done before to persuade Melba to take us forward to 2048 and not 1940? I wasn't even sure that this was possible.

What I did not want was for Brenda to return to 1940 and stay there as a nurse tending the wounded! With her there fulfilling her life-long dream of looking after handsome young soldiers anything could happen and I probably would never be able to talk her into helping me out. Maybe Melba was the key to success, but I couldn't see her without Brenda's help.

Malcolm J. Brooks

Where oh where had my powers gone? What had happened to my ability to time-travel at will and not be stuck in this terrible time-warp? Maybe somehow, I could reverse whatever had happened to me.

Giving myself up!

Much to the dismay of the three boys, I told them on the following Sunday night that I would take the bus down into the town and give myself up to the police.

"Why?" said Alan most dejectedly, "after all we have done for you?"
"I know and I'm very grateful for all you have done to help me escape from the police, but I am going to be caught eventually and it is better to give myself up rather than be found here. You three boys could get into trouble and maybe even end up with a police record which would have an effect on your lives for ever."

"She's right," said John, "we can't go on forever hiding Eva and she has to have her leg seen to eventually and I cannot see the doctors not informing the police."

"I did see those girls and give them your message," said Derek.

That wasn't really what I wanted to hear at this time.
"Yes, thank you. That was really good of you. My friend Bessie will be very pleased to hear that you spoke to them," I lied. "Look, I know that you are all disappointed that our little adventure is coming to an end, but I have given it a great deal of thought and it's best if I hand myself in to the police."

"We'll never forget you, Eva," John said with just a tinge of sadness in his voice.
"I hope you will," I muttered under my breath.
"I promise that I will come back and visit you later on, once all the trouble has died down. Don't you three say anything about the escape that you planned. It must remain a secret between us."

My promise of coming back would indeed happen. The year would be 2006, but it would be John who would visit me not the other way around; and I don't recall seeing Alan or Derek on that occasion.

I limped into the town's police station on the following Monday morning, the 28th January, and gave myself up. The very cold weather had passed for the time being and it was quite a warm day for January.

They didn't seem all that enthralled to see me. Whether this was because of all the paper-work they might have to do or that they had missed out on the excitement of tracking down a dangerous Russian spy, I wasn't quite sure.

Eva and the Winter of 63

"What did you say your name was?" The on-duty policeman asked. He was obviously not an avid watcher of the news.
I was a bit taken aback. "Eva Mills, Mrs Eva Mills."
"You say that you are wanted as a Russian spy?"
"Yes. Could I see PC Evans?"
"He's not on duty today."
"What about DI Rosebury or DI Bowers?"
"DI Bowers should be around."
"Can I speak to him?"
"Yes," and he reached for the phone and made a call.

There was something not quite right about this encounter. Surely every policeman in the area would know about me and my escape from the hospital.

DI Bowers arrived and with a bit more urgency than the policeman at the desk had shown ushered me into an interview room.
"Where have you been?"
"Hiding"
"Why?"
"Why? Because you lot think I'm a Russian spy."
"We've had a change of heart."
"What! What about all those news bulletins I watched declaring that you were looking for a dangerous Russian spy who should on no account be approached!"

"The boys in London thought that it was a bit over the top and called the search off."
"Nobody told me!"
"You were hiding and we couldn't find you!"
"What about Mr Wilson?"

"Who?"
"The man from MI whatever, you know, the secret service."
"What are you talking about?"

This was no longer funny. Something had happened and if I wasn't going to be interviewed by the high-powered guy from London, I wouldn't be assessed as mentally unstable by the very capable Dr Hawcutt and wouldn't be sectioned into Royd's Hall as someone who was a danger to the country!

"You can leave a free woman, Mrs Mills. We no longer think that you are dangerous."
"But I'm mentally unstable," I screamed.
This shook DI Bowers and in truth it shocked me.
"Now don't make a scene. Please leave or I will have to have you escorted from the premises."

I really don't know what came over me but I was desperate. This was not what was supposed to happen. I was supposed to have a meaningless interview with Mr Wilson where I tried to tell the truth and he didn't believe me and then a fun 'word association' test with Dr Hawcutt who would assign me to Royd's Hall for further observation!

I lashed out at DI Bowers like a deranged animal, swinging fists and kicking out with my pot leg. I know this is stupid to say now, but I had never been in a fight before so I didn't realise how painful punching and kicking someone could be, especially with a broken ankle.

Eva and the Winter of 63

DI Bowers was quite reasonable given his circumstances but I was 'escorted', for the want of a better word, to a cell in order for me to 'cool down'.

It did give me some time to think things through. I came to the conclusion that maybe the fact that I wasn't to be incarcerated in Royd's Hall and guarded 24/7 by a policeman wasn't as bad as I had first thought. After all, I knew where Royd's Hall was and since I was not going to be guarded it gave me a bit more freedom to do what I wanted.

I apologised to DI Bowers, and although I was given a caution concerning my attack on a policeman, I was released and free to leave. I did try to give some mitigating circumstances in that I had been 'on the run' and alone for some weeks with little sleep and things to eat. Not quite true but it was all I could come up with at the time.

I returned to the house of John's grandparents in order to think through a plan that might work. I wasn't expecting to do this so I had to retrieve the key from under the plant pot where I had hidden it. It must have been common practice to do this but not the most secure. There were a lot of differences between 1963 and 2048 and this was certainly one of them; home security didn't seem such an issue in 1963.

I listed the facts I knew to be correct:-

1. Brenda, although she didn't know it, had the same powers as I had had.
2. At this point, from her point of view, Brenda had never met me and when she did it would be as a visitor not an inmate of Royd's Hall.
3. Even though I could not see Melba the ghost, I knew where she hung out, so to speak.
4. I needed Brenda in order to see and talk to Melba.

And finally-

5. I needed both Melba and Brenda in order to get me home!

The other thing that was clear to me was that I needed to have the pot off my leg before I returned to 2048. This was due to happen six weeks after I had had the pot put on which by my reckoning was about 13th February, the day before Valentine's Day!
Therefore, I had two weeks in which to put any plan into action.

Back to Royd's Hall

I explained to the boys about what had happened when I gave myself up, and they laughed, partly due to my description of the attack on DI Bowers.

"I need to stay here a few days longer and make a few trips to Royd's Hall."
"Where exactly is that?" said Alan.
"Near Wakefield. I need to get the bus there but haven't got any money for the journeys. I wondered if there's any chance of borrowing some from you?"
"We don't have much," said Derek, "but there is another way to get some money. If the police have forgiven you maybe they will give you back all your possessions including the guns. You could sell them on the market on Saturday."

Derek's plan worked well, although I didn't get as much money as I would have got in 2048 even taking inflation into account. They managed to raise five pounds seven shillings and sixpence for the six guns, but it would cover my needs given that the boys still provided me with food. Since they had come clean about my whereabouts, Pearl, Sheila and Alan's Mum had been most generous and understanding of my plight although they must have been a little concerned about how long it would go on.

I had tried to reassure them all that once the pot had been removed from my leg I would go away for good. They kindly said that that wasn't necessary but I insisted that it was!

It was nice to hear about what the boys were going to do that Saturday evening when they brought me the money. According to Alan and John there were two programmes (which I assumed were on television) called 'Thank Your Lucky Stars' and 'Juke Box Jury' which were going to be special that evening. The first programme was going to be a real spectacular as it was to include Jess Conrad, John Leyton, Jo Brown and Brian Hyland, whilst 'Juke Box Jury' had Mike Sarne appearing. I had to admit to the boys that I had never heard of any of them. I could have mentioned the groups from the 2040s such as The Skunks, Tangerine Pineapple, Zynerz and my favourite band The Barking Bubbles. Of course there were still old stagers like Bruno Mars and Olly Murs who were now both nearly sixty.

On Sunday 3rd February I made my first visit to Royd's Hall, well my first visit in this cycle of events. Things were getting so complicated with the three times I had returned to Sledger's Hill and received a broken ankle that I had to try hard to remember what I should know and what I shouldn't.

Although I arrived as a new visitor I did have an insight from my previous time as a patient as to who would be the best person to ask to see. That person was Ian Robinson, a kindly man who sadly was in the latter stages of Alzheimer's disease. At that time the label wasn't in general use and he was regarded as someone who was senile. In 2048 Alzheimer's disease had been eradicated with drugs to slow down the ageing process. Yes, people became forgetful as they grew older but the bizarre behaviour associated with Alzheimer's could be regulated with injections and tablets.

I asked to see Ian and was told that he would be brought down to the dayroom and that I should wait there for him to arrive. After twenty minutes, a nurse and a bewildered Ian approached and sat down next to me. I felt ashamed that I was involving Ian in my plan but I needed to spend some time in Royd's Hall in order to speak to Brenda.

The conversation between the three of us was forced and all the time I was keeping one eye on the whereabouts of Brenda. As yet I had not seen her. Normally her family met her in the dayroom but neither they nor she were in evidence at the moment. Suddenly, down the stairs to the right of where we sat, Brenda appeared followed by a lady I knew to be her mother. As usual no words passed between them. I turned to the nurse and said, "I'm sorry I must go now. It's been nice talking to you, Ian."

He muttered something inaudible and the nurse smiled. "Thank you for coming to see Ian, he doesn't get many visitors."

I rose and turned towards the door just as Brenda and her mother passed by. I was tempted to say something there and then but at the last moment thought it unwise with her mother present. I needed to have my conversation with Brenda on her own. At least I was confident that I would get a positive reaction from her, as I had before.

In a pre-planned move I had left the umbrella I had been carrying in the dayroom. I had put it under the chair on which I had been sitting so that the nurse wouldn't see it as I left. Once outside, I waited for Brenda's Mum to pass me before re-entering the hall.

Brenda was half-way up the stairs, presumably going back to her room. Without retrieving the umbrella I quickly followed her upstairs, hoping no-one had noticed my speedy return through the dayroom. I caught up with her on the second flight of stairs leading to her second floor room. She jumped a little as I touched her arm.

"Hello, you don't know me. I'm Eva Mills."
Her response threw me.
"Oh yes, of course I know you. I've been waiting for you to contact me."

Eva and the Winter of 63

"But we've never met!"
"Yes, I know but Melba said that you'd be coming to talk to me."
I was stunned into silence for a moment.
"Melba said that a lady called Eva would come and tell me about my powers because she had the same powers as me, and here you are. Shall we go to my room and have a chat."

I meekly followed her to her room. My mind was swimming with this unusual turn of events. Once inside her room I had recovered sufficiently enough to ask her exactly what Melba had said.

"She said that you would be shocked when I said I was waiting for you, but that you were a nice lady who wanted to help me get out of this place."
"She didn't tell you how it could be done?"
"No, she said it would be best if you showed me what was possible with my special powers. What are these special powers Eva, apart from being able to see people who have died?"

I had to be careful. My plan was to stop her going back to 1940 and becoming a nurse too soon. I needed Melba's help to go forward in time not back.

"Well, Brenda, you and I indeed have special powers. We can travel through time, that is provided the ghosts we can see allow us to."
"Wow, travel through time!" she gasped, "that sounds like fun."

"Yes, it can be but at times it is quite scary so you must use the power wisely."
"How have you used it, Eva?"
"Well, when I was eleven I met a man called John and he was the first person to believe me when I said I could see people who had died. We met a ghost called Valentine Walton in a church near here and he was so sad that he had been killed before he had had chance to see his son, who was also called Valentine."
"What did you do?"
"John didn't want to, but I persuaded him to come with me back into the 17th century and get Valentine's son so he could see him."

"Did it work?"
"Well yes and no. We brought the young Valentine back for his father to see, but poor John got arrested for kidnapping me and the baby. That's why I said that you have to be careful."
"Did he go to prison?"
"He was found guilty and sentenced to many years in prison but I managed to help him escape."
"How did you do that?"
"It's a long story but it meant another trip back to the 17th century. We did manage to take the young Valentine back to his mother but it was really dangerous."

"Sounds exciting!"
"It was in a way. Anyway, can I talk to Melba please?"
"You can see her for yourself, can't you?"
"Thereby hangs a problem, Brenda. Something has happened and I don't seem to be able to see all ghosts now, just some of them. Could you do me a favour?"

Eva and the Winter of 63

"Yes, of course.
"I need to talk to Melba."
"About what?"
"About me getting back home."
"You don't live around here?"
"Yes I do but not at this time. I've come from 2048."
"Wow! What's it like then?"
"Let's just say it's different. I can explain later. Can we go see Melba now?"
"It depends if she is around. She's not always on the landing. She must go to other places to haunt people."

"How are you and your family?"
"You know about that?"
"I observed that you and your mother didn't seem, what shall I say, on the best of terms."
"She thinks I'm mad, seeing ghosts all the time. That's why she had me put in this place, but I am not mad, am I Eva?"
"No, definitely not Brenda, definitely not. Let's go see Melba, shall we?"

Sadly the landing was a ghost-free area, so I said goodbye to Brenda and we agreed to meet the following day at 4pm after the official visiting time. Brenda said that she would try and see Melba and arrange for her to be present at 4pm.

Meeting Melba again

I arrived in good time at Royd's Hall the following day but decided that it would be unfair to see Ian again. I was only using him as a means of seeing Brenda and that wasn't right.

I decided to wait outside until Brenda's family had departed. This time it seemed to be her sister that had got the 'visit Brenda' duty. It seemed such a shame that Brenda's special powers were treated in such a negative manner. It had happened to me to some extent before John arrived but I was never locked away in a home for people with 'mental problems'.

Brenda was waiting for me. She had managed to get rid of her visitors slightly earlier than usual and was at the door to meet me.
"She's upstairs," she whispered and we climbed the stairs to the second landing.

Eva and the Winter of 63

I took Brenda's hand. She looked surprised initially and then realized why I had done it. Although previously Melba had been described to me by Brenda as old, in fact she was probably about my age.

Melba was the first to speak. "I hear you want to talk to me because I might be able to help you."
Was there just a hint of malice in her voice or was I getting a bit more neurotic?
"Yes, I would like you and Brenda to please take me back to 2048, to somewhere near where I live."
"That's quite a favour to ask someone."
"Yes, I suppose it is."
"What will you do in return for me?"
"I don't understand what you mean."
"One good deed deserves another, Eva, doesn't it?"
"Yes, I suppose it does. What could I possibly do for you though Melba?"
"That's easy, Eva. Find out who murdered me and bring them to justice. Then I will take you home!"

"You were murdered!" interjected Brenda.
"Yes, I was. They all thought that it was a heart attack but I believe someone was poisoning me."
"Why would anybody want to do that?"
"The most obvious reason is money," replied Melba.
"Wouldn't they have found poison in your body at the autopsy?" I asked the obvious question.
"They were too busy to have an autopsy. With all those injured and dying soldiers coming back from Dunkirk they didn't bother with a so called 'mad woman' in a home who'd died of a suspected heart attack."

"Do you have any idea who would do such a thing, Melba?" I asked.
"Yes, but I don't want to hinder your investigation."
"My investigation?"
"Well, yours and Brenda's. You can't do it without Brenda."
At this Brenda became very excited. "Oh yes, I would love to be a detective like that Parrot that Agatha Christie writes about."
"I think that you mean Poirot," corrected Melba.
"That's him. He was a French detective."
"Belgian, actually," came Melba's second correction.
"Oh yes, Belgian."

"So let me get this straight Melba. If I find out who murdered you in 1940 and get them convicted, then you will take me home?"
"That's about the size of it."
"Can you give me anything to go on?"
"Not really. You need to return to 1940 on the day I died and work it out from there."
"How do we go back to 1940?" asked Brenda.
"That's the easy bit," I replied, rather disgruntled at the size of the task facing my return home.
"Are you going to start now?"
"No, I need to have this plaster removed from my leg. I don't want to return home with it on and it would certainly hamper any detective work I might want to do." I had resigned myself to the fact that, at least, this was a possible way out of my time-warp.

"You could always get them to remove it in 1940. There are plenty of men with 'pots' on in Royd's Hall back in

1940 as this place became a temporary hospital," said Melba trying to be helpful.
"Why are you in such a hurry?"
"No reason."
"I have a question for you."
"Fire away!"
"Did you have anything to do with the fact that the police were not looking for me when I gave myself up?"
"Might have."
"Why?"
"I wanted you back here without any guards and questions about where you were and what you were doing."
"Why me?"
"You're a nobody. You don't exist here in 1963 nor in 1940. You can do what you want and nobody knows who you are and where you have come from except me and Brenda."

"I'm the ideal person to solve a murder?"
"Yes, you are intelligent, resourceful and have knowledge from the future. I realized that from the first moment I saw you."
"You've met before?" enquired Brenda.
For the first time that day Melba and I smiled.
"Yes, we have."
If Brenda was expecting an explanation she didn't get one.

The murder of Melba Bartle

"Before we go back to the scene of your death, can you tell us anything at all?" I enquired.
Before Melba had the chance to reply, Brenda said, "We can go back to the past?"
I was tempted to say 'Yes, you've done it once before' but decided to follow my line of enquiry with Melba.
"There must be something that you can tell us about the circumstances of your death."
"Only that I began feeling unwell two weeks before I died and the pains I kept getting were always in the evenings."

"Did you see a doctor?"
"Yes, but he just told me that I had probably strained something. I think he thought that I was exaggerating to get sympathy."
"Did you used to do things like that?"
"Of course not, I'm no drama-queen!"

Eva and the Winter of 63

"OK, anything else?"
"No, not really. Oh, there was one thing. After the Dunkirk evacuation at the start of June, lots of medical staff began to arrive and with them lots of medical supplies came in lorries. They had no real place to keep them securely locked up so they used an office near the kitchens. Then the soldiers, poor things began to arrive and they made some of the larger rooms into temporary operating theatres. Many of the residents were returned to their relatives to make way for the injured soldiers. I was due to go and live with my sister Jane. Some people made it clear that they were not pleased to have their 'mad' relative come to stay with them."
"What about your sister Jane? Was she pleased to be getting you to share her home?"
"I think that she was OK about it. At least she didn't say anything to the contrary. I'm not sure that her husband Fred was too keen about it though."

I was surprised that Brenda didn't remember going down Melba's 'corridor of transit' before, but then again there were lots of things I did not understand about time. I had read that if we were able to travel quickly enough to some of the distant planets then it was possibly only the middle-ages there.

The next few minutes went exactly as it had done the first time. The familiar bright lights and tunnel were soon surrounding us, well familiar that is to me. Poor Brenda looked a little nervous again.

Soon we were in the same corridor where we had started.

"Nothing has happened," said Brenda.
"Oh yes, it has!"
There were voices coming from downstairs. "Melba's fallen; I think that she might be dead! Quick, get the doctor!"

There again, before us, was a prone Melba and at the side of her body was the ghostly version of the same woman.
"Quick, get into that room!"
I pulled a bewildered Brenda into the room that Melba had indicated and closed the door.

"What's going on? I don't understand," she said.
"Shush. They'll hear you."
"Who will?"
"Let me explain what has happened," I whispered. "We are still in Royd's Hall and on the second floor but it's the year 1940. I'm not sure what date it is because it's the day Melba died."

The conversation went the same way as it had the first time that we were in Melba's room.

"I still don't understand. This is not my room. Look at all the strange ornaments, although the curtains, carpets and even the wall paper appear to be the same."
"I don't know whether this is your room or not, but as I said, the year is 1940!"
"Why 1940?"
"Didn't you hear Melba say that she had died in 1940? Didn't you notice that there were two Melbas out there? There was the dead one on the floor where she had

Eva and the Winter of 63

presumably just fallen and the . . ." I hesitated because I was just about to say 'live' one, "and the ghost one who spoke to us!"

"How do you know that the one on the floor was Melba? I couldn't see her face."
"Well, one 'corridor of transit' of all ghosts leads them to the place and time they died. Melba chose that one for us to walk down. If it had been the time and place of her birth we would have seen her as a baby."

This time however, I had to spell out clearly what we must do. I didn't want her to see that this was just a 'Florence Nightingale' expedition. What she would do after I went home was up to her, but whilst here I had to be selfish and in charge.

"Look Brenda, we're here on a mission to find Melba's murderer and for no other reason!"
"But . . ."
"Out there, there are lots of wounded soldiers coming back from Dunkirk. We're going to pretend that we are nurses, whilst we do our investigating."
"How do you know all that?"
"Because I've been here before." I didn't want to add to the confusion by saying 'and so have you'.

"They're in the process of converting this 'home' into a military hospital. We're going to offer our services as nurses."
"This is all very exciting, but have you ever been a nurse?"
"No, neither have you, but we won't let a little thing like that worry us."

"I've spent nearly all my life watching nurses at the home and I know what they do."

"This might be a different type of nursing. There will be lots of blood and horrible injuries that you've never seen before, but I know that you will cope well. You are a strong person Brenda, despite what has happened to you."

She smiled. "I like you, Eva. We are going to be good friends."
"And nurses!"
"Yes and nurses."
"What are we going to do now?"
"Exactly as we did the first time! Walk down the stairs and out of the front door into the garden."
"The first time?"
"Never mind, we need our nurses' uniforms and I know where we can get them."

In the garden, we again saw numerous soldiers with the injuries they had received at Dunkirk. We were lucky that, in the main, these were not life-threatening injuries but the shock of being part of such a traumatic retreat in the face of the German onslaught must have left the soldiers with many inward scars that would be with them for many years to come.

All went just as it had before. We met the lovely lads from Sussex and made our presence known to the people in charge. The only deviation from before was that with my pot leg I needed to take a more leading role in explaining how we had been sent there and it was me that collected the uniforms and not Brenda. Everything of course that I told them was a lie but in the confusion of creating a make-shift hospital and the influx of so many soldiers, they believed everything I said, even down to the way I got my injury playing football!

Melba's death was sadly just a passing foot-note of the day, when more important things were happening. It was no use thinking too much about 'the murder' that day. We were thrown into the ravages of war. However, I did make some enquires later in the afternoon about where they had taken Melba's body.

"To the morgue in Wakefield."
"Have any of Melba's family been informed?"
"I'm not sure," came the reply.

With the influx of so many soldiers, the place was in chaos. This was to the murderer's advantage but it did allow me to move around without too many questions being asked.

Whether I could spare the time to visit the morgue and also maybe speak to the doctor who had signed the death certificate, was debatable.

Brenda was in seventh heaven. She now had the life she wanted. Nobody thought of her as mad and she could care for people in a way that no-one had ever cared for her.

During breaks between duties, I tried to explain to her the dangers of time-travelling since she seemed oblivious to them.

"You can't mention anything about 1963 or even anything that has happened since 1940. Do you understand?"
"Yes, of course," she said as if in a day-dream.
"You can't mention anything about the King dying, or the Coronation of Queen Elizabeth, the birth of Charles and Anne and, I stress this most of all, you cannot say anything about who won the war!"
I almost shouted these last few words as if to wake her up.

She smiled, "I understand, Eva."
"If you do, they will try to lock you up as they did with me for being a Russian spy."
"You mean a German spy!"
"Yes, I suppose I do. Nowadays they would think that spies are German. Funny how time changes how one country perceives another! You aren't wearing anything that's been bought for you recently, are you?"
"Only my watch that I got for my last birthday and this ring and necklace."

"I don't really know if they are any different from now but just to be on the safe side, take them off, just as I have done."
"OK," she agreed, "at least we have Melba as an escape route, even if we haven't caught the murderer."

Since I had told the very harassed organiser that we didn't live nearby and had been assigned from a

Eva and the Winter of 63

hospital further south, we were billeted in a small room in the attic of the house.

"I never knew these rooms existed," said Brenda.
"Probably in 1963 they didn't! They look like the kind of rooms that servants were given in the days when this house was a mansion for a rich family."
"It will be nice sharing a room with you."
I smiled weakly as I wasn't too sure about how true this might be.
With all the stairs up to the room my leg was beginning to ache.
"I must ask them to remove this 'pot'. It must be about time."
"I could do it for you now, if you want?"
"Could you?" I asked dubiously.
"Yes. I borrowed these large scissors from one of the medical kits just for that very reason," and she produced an enormous set of cutters!
"Wow! That's really thoughtful of you, Brenda."
"We're going to be the best of friends," and with that, she began cutting away at the pot. It took some time but was a great relief. The skin beneath the pot looked pale and wizened; it also smelled quite a bit! When I first stood up without the pot on, I was a bit unsteady on my feet as I staggered rather than walked around the small room.

The room had two single beds, a cupboard and a set of drawers for clothes but sadly no 'en-suite'. You couldn't swing the proverbial cat around! The nearest toilet and washroom were on the floor below, but at least it gave me the chance to practice walking without a pot.

Whilst Brenda threw herself wholeheartedly into her daily routine, I did find the time to do a little investigating. By that I mean I talked to the patients and resident staff who knew Melba and were present at the time of her death. The Matron and some of the nurses painted a picture of Melba as a 'batty old lady' who was for ever complaining about things. With the fact that she was only fifty-three years old when she died, it did seem a bit harsh to call her old. She was the same age as me!

"Someone has stolen my favourite ornament."
"Money has gone missing from my room."
"I feel very ill. I'm being poisoned."

These were some of the things that Melba was alleged to have said.
"She had a very vivid imagination did our Melba," one of the nurses had said.
"What about her relatives? Did they say that things had gone missing?" I had asked.
"No, not really. There was only her sister and her husband, oh, and their daughter. Both her parents were dead. There was one old chap who used to visit her. What was he called? Oh yes, she said his name was Jean-Pierre and that he was French. Fought in the Great War."

None of this information gave any clue as to who the murderer was, but at least there were people I could try and talk to.

Eva and the Winter of 63

What would a real detective like Hercule Poirot do?

Whilst on a rare break from nursing duties, I wrote down a list of motives and potential suspects:-

Motives:
Money
Jealousy
Hatred
Blackmail
Rage

To my mind, these were the things for which people killed. If Melba was right, it was pre-meditated poisoning, so rage was off the list.

The list of suspects was long:

Her sister Jane
Her brother-in-law (name as yet unknown)
Her niece (name also unknown)
The Matron
Any nurse
Any inmate of the home

Oh yes, and the mysterious Jean-Pierre. If only I could speak to him, maybe Melba had confided in him about her suspicions. Did Jean-Pierre know Melba was dead? Would he visit the hospital again?

The answer to the last question was answered two days later. Brenda and I were busy taking two soldiers for 'walks' in their old-fashioned, hard to push, wheel-chairs. It seemed to be the height of summer, with 'wall to wall' sunshine in the garden.

Despite their injuries, the soldiers were very chatty and although, as a middle-aged married woman, I didn't attract much of their attention, Brenda did, and she loved it. I cannot blame her. She was pretty in a quirky sort of way, but in the role of carer, she was perfect. Nothing was too much trouble and her patients appreciated her loving and caring approach.

I saw him at the end of the drive and there was something typically French about him. No, he wasn't wearing a beret and hooped jumper, nor did he have a garland of onions around his neck and he definitely wasn't riding a bicycle, but there was something French about the way that he held himself, proud and upright. If he had fought in the First World War he must have been about my age or maybe a little younger, but he looked very slim and fit for his age.

"Just a moment Brenda, can we rest here for a few minutes? I want to go and talk to that man over there."
"No problem," came the reply. She had learned that reply from me as I was pretty sure it wasn't a 1960's saying.

I caught up with the man as he approached the main entrance.
"Jean-Pierre!" I called.
He turned and in an accent that had a slight French lilt he said. "Do I know you?"
"No, I don't think you do, but I'm Eva, a friend of Melba's."

Eva and the Winter of 63

"Oh, it is her that I have come to see."
"Can we go in and sit down for a moment. There's something I must tell you."

He took the news of Melba's death with stoical grace and what he said next came as no surprise.
"Mon dieu! She said that someone was poisoning her, but I didn't believe her and now she is dead. I should have done or said something!" He seemed genuinely upset at his lack of action in the matter.

"Did she say anything about the suspicions she had as to who might have done such a thing?"
"Non pas de tout. She was a little prone to exaggeration."
"So you didn't believe her at all?"
"No, and now she is dead!"
"What about her family? Did you know them at all?"
"Not really. Her sister, Jane is a very nice woman. She visited Melba regularly and I met her when our visits coincided. It was the intention that Melba would go and stay with her in Harrogate for the duration of the war. They were trying to remove all the patients from the Hall ready for the arrival of the injured soldiers."

"Did Melba like the prospect of going to live with Jane?"
"Yes and no. Jane and her got on well, despite her little . . . ."
"Idiosyncrasies?"
"My English is not perfect, but that seems to be the word."
"Your English seems excellent to me. How long have you lived here?"
"Since the end of the Great War. I came here in 1918."

"Where did you first meet Melba?"
"I had had an accident and an enforced stay in a hospital in London. Melba was a nurse there and we became good friends as I convalesced. That was in 1926 and we have been friends ever since, although only as, how do you say, 'writing friends' as she moved north when she married Albert."
"We call them 'pen friends'."
"Ah oui, 'pen friends'. I was very surprised when she wrote to me to say that she had been forced to live here in Royd's Hall. She didn't enjoy living here but with her husband dying so dramatically and her illness, it seemed the best place for her to be. Sadly that proved to be so wrong."

"How did her husband die?"
"She said it was a car accident."
"And what was Melba's illness."
"I'm not sure of its exact name but the tragic death of Albert had an effect on her mind."
"Do you think Melba was murdered?"
"I really don't think so."
"Could you do me a favour?"
"Oui, bien sur. What do you want me to do?"
"Well, it's difficult for me to leave this place. All the nurses are working so hard and we don't get too much time off. Could you find out where they have taken Melba's body? It's important to find out if she was in fact poisoned and what the poison was. You may need to go to the police with Melba's suspicions and see if you can get an autopsy carried out."
"An autopsy?"

Eva and the Winter of 63

"Yes, it means that they try to find out the cause of death."

"Ah, bien. I will try but whether they listen to me. I do have a friend who is a solicitor. Perhaps he might know the best thing to do."

"The Matron said that she thought Melba's body had been taken to the morgue in Wakefield, but she wasn't too sure."

We talked for a bit more about his life in France prior to the First World War and then about his time in the war. Then he left with a promise to return to let me know if he had found anything of importance.

Poisonous intent

It was about a week before Jean-Pierre returned. During that time Brenda and I worked as hard as we could to make the soldiers comfortable. There were other nurses but it was clear that there were as yet, not enough of us to deal with the constant influx of wounded soldiers. We also had several over-worked doctors who seemed to work around the clock, either in the temporary theatres or doing daily rounds as their patients had rest and recuperation.

Sadly, a number of soldiers died from their wounds mainly from secondary infections that occurred in the make-shift hospital.

Since Jean-Pierre didn't know when I would be free to talk, he must have waited quite a time for my appearance in the entrance hall.

Eva and the Winter of 63

"I'm sorry, I only have about ten minutes to spare," I said hurriedly as I saw him sitting there.
"I have some news which might be of some importance."
"Fire away."
"Pardon? I do not understand."
"I mean please tell me what you've found out."
"She died of mercury poisoning. Quite an amount of it was found in her body. They said that it seems to have occurred over a period of time."
"Are the police going to investigate?"
"I doubt it. They don't seem to have the time to investigate such a death. They say that they have much more pressing problems to deal with."
"Letting someone get away with murder!"
"It seems that way. Are you going to do anything? Investigate, I mean."
"Yes, it's very important that I find out who murdered Melba. At least I can tell her that her suspicions were right and that she was poisoned."

Jean-Pierre looked at me in astonishment.
"She is dead! How can you possibly tell her?"
"Sorry, I've been working so hard, I don't know what I'm saying!"

We briefly talked about the funeral plans that Jane had arranged. She had, for some reason, contacted him with the details, which seemed strange given that Jean-Pierre had seemed to infer that they did not know each other that well.

Eventually, I made my apologies for the fact I wouldn't be able to attend the funeral and we said our good-byes.

Brenda was the apple of many a soldiers' eye and, it might be said, was handling their advances with a degree of maturity that I hadn't expected, given her life in a home with very little male contact.

One particular soldier that we had met on our first day appeared smitten by Brenda. His name was Jack and he was one of the soldiers who hailed from Eastbourne. What interested me was that, prior to being conscripted into the Royal Engineers, he had just become a teacher, and what's more, a science teacher!

One morning Brenda and I were again doing our 'walking duties' with Jack and another Royal Engineer from Eastbourne called Henry.

"Do you know anything about mercury poisoning, Jack?"
"Mercury poisoning? What do you want to know about that for?"
"Just interested in something I read in the paper this morning that said eating fish can cause mercury poisoning," I lied.
"Mercury is very toxic and must be handled carefully, but it has lots of uses, for example, those thermometers you nurses use are full of the stuff."
"Why is eating fish a problem?"
"There's evidence that quite a lot of the oceans are polluted with mercury and apparently mercury poisoning has been caused by eating tuna fish."
"Tuna fish?"

Eva and the Winter of 63

"Yes, I'm not sure why tuna are more susceptible to being the carriers of such a poison."

A short time later, I made my way to the kitchen to ask the obvious question. The cook I asked was busy but she assured me that they weren't in a position yet to afford such a luxury as tuna.
"There is a war on, you know."

I made my apologies and left.
Mercury poisoning by tuna fish didn't seem to be the murderer's most obvious weapon. It was a line of enquiry which I felt was unlikely but it had to be checked out. If it had been the cause of Melba's demise we would be dealing with multiple deaths, not just that of Melba.

However, when the opportunity arose, I got Brenda to check with Melba that she hadn't eaten tuna fish in any large quantities.

Apparently, it took some days before Brenda had the chance to talk to Melba. Brenda reported back that Melba was a bit angry at my insinuation that her death could have been caused by her eating too much tuna! She hated the stuff!

The days turned into weeks and the time I had for investigating purposes seemed to diminish as the causalities from Dunkirk increased. We were successful in rehabilitating many soldiers either back to their homes or back to their regiments.

Jean-Pierre turned up unexpectedly one afternoon to see how my investigations were coming along. He seemed disappointed at my progress.

"I do have some information."
"Yes?"
"The motive wasn't money. She hardly had any left. Her sister inherited all that she possessed, but it wasn't worth committing murder for."
"Thanks Jean-Pierre. Have you any more news?"
"Not really news but thoughts of what might have happened."
"I'm listening."
"Mercury poisoning can be administered in a number of ways, and from what Melba said, she felt that it had been done over a period of time."

"It cannot have been as a result of what she had eaten. She didn't eat tuna. She hated the stuff. If it had been fish that was the source of the poison, others would have been affected too."
"I agree, so the mercury must have been put into her body in some other way."
"How?"
"She told me once that she had had some dental work done, so I did some research. Mercury is used in the fillings that are used to repair the damage and decay to teeth."
"I don't follow you. You mean her dentist did it?"
"No, no but it might be the reason why they found so much mercury in her system. She told me that she had to keep going back to the dentist because her fillings kept falling out. Maybe she swallowed them?"

"In other words, we are barking up the wrong tree?"
"Pardon, I don't understand what you mean. My English . . ."
"No, it's my fault. You must have things, sayings, in French that don't really mean what they appear to mean."

"Mais oui, for example we have a saying 'quand les poules auront des dents' which literally means 'when chicken will have teeth' but is used to mean it will never happen."
"A bit like 'pigs might fly'."
"Oui, c'est ça."
"Ok, what I was saying was that if mercury was the poison that killed Melba then it wasn't murder. It was an accident from the many visits to the dentist and bad fillings!"
"Yes, it's how you English say; the idea she had about being murdered by poison was 'a red herring'."
"Very good, Jean-Pierre. It is a red herring and we are back at square one."
"Square one?"
"Back at the start of our murder investigations."
"But we have ruled out murder now haven't we?"
"Maybe, we need to look for another motive and another means of murder."
"I do not think it was murder. Money is not the motive, she had little left, and there seems to be no other reason for her death apart from accidental poisoning."
He seemed so certain that I had to agree.

"There was one thing at the funeral that was odd."
"Yes, what was that?"

"Jane's husband Fred didn't turn up."
"Maybe he was working?"
"I think he is a retired Chemist, so unless he is doing some part-time work you would have thought that he would have been present."
"Did anybody say anything about his absence?"
"Only that he was not very fond of his sister-in-law as you English call them."
"OK. Anyway I must get back to work. These soldiers won't heal themselves!" A particularly stupid thing to say as most of the healing process would take place after surgery whilst they rested.

"I will come back and see you next week."
"Bye."
"Au revoir, Eva!"

We appeared to be winning the battle as there came a time when more soldiers were leaving for rehabilitation elsewhere than were arriving. In the main we were dealing with wounds to non-vital limbs and organs, from gunshot or shrapnel.

I hadn't had time to see Melba for a couple of weeks and was a bit reluctant to do so after my 'tuna fish' mistake. However, I needed to ask her a few questions and so organised Brenda to meet me on the second floor landing when we had the same break for lunch.

The usual hand-holding routine put me in touch with Melba.

"Did you get on with your brother-in-law, Fred?"
"That stupid man! No, I did not. He was a buffoon! I don't see what Jane saw in him, only that he had a Chemistry degree from some lesser University."
"The other thing is about your visits to the dentists."
"How do you know about those?"
"Jean-Pierre told me."
"You've met J-P?"
"Yes, he seems a really nice man."
"Should have married him!"
"I'm already married," I teased her.
"Not you. I should have married him back in 1926 when I had the chance."
"He asked you to marry him?"
"Yes, but I said 'no'."
"Why?"
"I was a nurse and I thought that he only liked me because I had nursed him through his illness. It happens a lot with the nurse-patient relationships. After I said 'no', J-P asked my sister to go out with him, sort of on the rebound."
"Did he?"
"Yes, came as quite a surprise to both Jane and me."

"Anyway, what about the dentists?"
"Had some fillings done, that's all."
"How many?"
"I had to go back because the fillings fell out twice. They're all right now."

A ghost telling me that her teeth are alright now!
"What happened to the fillings that dropped out?"

"I swallowed one of them! I assume it came out through my system so to speak."
"I guess it would."

Do you still need to go to the toilet when you are dead?
"I don't know what happened to the other filling," she concluded.

I had got all the information I needed for the time being. The increased levels of mercury in Melba's body and her feeling that she was being poisoned had a logical explanation, but it wasn't anything to do with murder.

"Oh, just one more question," I said as I was about to let go of Brenda's hand, "did you ever have any heart trouble?"
"No, never! Strong as an ox my heart was."

As I turned back along the landing, I noticed a nurse looking around the corner leading to the stairs. She disappeared quickly and by the time I got to the stairs she was nowhere to be seen. It seemed strange behaviour but maybe seeing two nurses talking to someone she couldn't see and not hearing any responses to the questions that were being asked, might have caused her to hide.

I didn't think anymore about it and maybe it wasn't wise to seek out the nurse as she might have had a few awkward questions for Brenda and me.

Eva and the Winter of 63

I lay awake that night, churning things over in my mind whilst Brenda 'purred' rhythmically in the other bed. I say 'purred' because 'snored' wouldn't have been the right description. 'Snoring' would irritate me, but her 'purring' didn't. It was quite soothing!

If mercury poisoning wasn't the reason for Melba's death then we were not necessarily looking at her being poisoned over a period of time. In fact we weren't looking at poisoning at all as the means of murder, if that indeed was what it was!

We might even be looking at an action that took place that day that instantly killed Melba. A blow to the head maybe? It couldn't have been that though as Melba would have known and remembered that it had happened. It wasn't, she said, a heart attack, although I suppose many people believe their heart is strong until an attack suddenly occurs.

What else would kill a person instantly and yet the person being killed would not be aware of what had happened?

I drifted off into dreamland with that question unanswered.

The next day I crossed out 'money' from my list of motives and put 'rage' back on to it! I crossed Melba's sister's name off my list but kept her husband's on, writing 'Fred' beside the crossed out parenthesis that had indicated that his name wasn't known. I also crossed off the name of Jean-Pierre, the mysterious Frenchman.

When I next saw Jean-Pierre, I had a small list of questions for him.
"What's Jane's and Fred's daughter like?"
"Très joli, very nice. She is a lovely girl, beautiful eyes and such a lovely temperament. She is only ten years old but one day she will make some lucky man a wonderful wife. No man will truly deserve such a woman."

With that glowing reference, I mentally crossed her off my list of suspects.
"What is her name?"
"Judy. Same as the famous American film star Judy Garland, although I don't think that was her real name. Do you remember her in the 'Wizard of Oz'?"

I had to confess that I'd never heard of the film or Judy Garland and this rather shocked him somewhat.
"Oh, but surely you have heard of Judy Garland?"
"Sorry. I don't go to see films very often."

In fact the last film I saw was when I took the children to see 'Night Garden 7' and there was nobody called Judy Garland in that film as it was a 3D animated film with Iggle Piggle, Makka Pakka and Upsy Daisy in the starring roles. I don't think Jean-Pierre would have understood the language they used. I certainly didn't, but the children loved it.

Eva and the Winter of 63

"How well do you know Jane and Fred?"
I sensed that he blushed a little. "I told you, not very well. We met a few times only. Of course, I met Jane again at the funeral."
"That doesn't seem to be the whole truth Jean-Pierre, does it? Surely, when you asked Melba to marry you, you were aware that she had a sister."
He looked uncomfortable. "Yes."
"Did you meet her when you were courting Melba?"
"No. She didn't live in London."

I knew that he was lying but it could hardly have anything to do with Melba's death. Suddenly he blurted it out.
"I asked Melba to marry me but when she refused, I asked her sister out. A bit of, how you say, spite. I did not love Jane as I had done Melba but we went out for a time and then we parted company. It was then she met Fred. He ran the town's Chemist shop and she went to work there. She is a bit younger than he is, about eight years I think."

"How old are you, Jean-Pierre?"
"Born in '95."
"So was I." I then realised my mistake. He was born in 1895 and I a century later in 1995.

―――

It was back to work when Jean-Pierre left and another round of 'goffering' for items required by doctors and patients alike.

Most of what I did, or more accurately, was given to do was low-level nursing. Someone must have realized that I was not highly-trained whereas Brenda seemed to have won the admiration of all for her efficiency and compassion. The transformation from the human being that I had first seen in the dayroom of Royd's Hall to 'super' nurse was incredible.

Whilst fetching yet another bedpan that evening, I noticed the nurse that I had seen watching Brenda and me talking to Melba on the second floor landing.

Something told me that I needed to talk to her as soon as possible. I delivered my bedpan and returned to where I had seen her, but she had disappeared. I looked for her as long as I dared and then returned to my duties.

I thought that it was strange that because she had seen me she had decided to hide. Maybe it was just a coincidence that she had to leave to be elsewhere. She couldn't hide for ever.

She didn't. The following day she literally ran straight into me.
"Sorry," she said and then she realized who she had bumped into. She looked embarrassed. So I took the initiative.
"I came to see you yesterday but I couldn't find you."

"Why would you want to see me?"
"You know why!"
"No, I don't."

"You were listening to Brenda and me talking on the landing. You were hiding and quickly disappeared when I saw you. Didn't you?" I was being slightly aggressive.
"I suppose I did," she relented.
"Why?"
"It's a long story."
"I'm listening."
"Can we go somewhere private?"
"Yes, do you have a room?"
"No, I live locally and come here every day on the bus."

"Follow me!"
We climbed the many stairs to my room.
"We haven't got long," she said, "I need to be back on the ward in ten minutes."
"OK, what's your story?"
"I'm Natalie. I worked as a nurse here before the soldiers began to arrive. I knew Melba well and was with her the morning she died."
"Was murdered, you mean."
"Murdered?"
"Yes, that's what she said."
"Sorry, who said?"
Oops! Quick thinking required.
"Brenda, my friend. The nurse you saw talking to me."
"Well, I'm not sure how or why she died, but I do know that she had a visitor that morning. In fact, she had two."

"Do you know who they were?"
"One was that Frenchman that used to come regularly to see her."
"And the other?"

"I had never seen him before."
"Why did you hide from me if this is all you know about her death?"

She hesitated.
"Because it might have been me that killed her!"
"Why do you think that?"
"It was a complete accident," she hesitated yet again. "I was taking her temperature. I had just inserted the thermometer under her tongue and it broke! The mercury went everywhere and I think she swallowed quite a bit of it. I heard you talking to Brenda about mercury poisoning on the landing and I was really scared that if people found out that I caused her death, I would lose my job or even worse, I could even be sent to prison for my carelessness."

"It wasn't your fault that the thermometer broke."
"But it was my fault that I didn't tell anyone who might then have been able to help her and maybe save her life."
"Did the accident occur before the two men visited Melba or after?"
"Before, but it takes time for mercury poisoning to take effect. I looked it up in one of the medical books we have at the Hall."

"I suppose that it's possible that the accident was the reason for Melba's death but it was an accident and you shouldn't worry about it, although you should have told someone about the accident."
"Yes, you're right, I have been stupid."
"Do you remember which of the visitors came first?"

"I couldn't say for certain."
"Not to worry. I do know someone who will remember for certain."

I wasn't going to tell her that it was Melba herself.
"I'd better go back to work."
"Me too," and with that we parted company.

Finding the answer

I had been so involved in my work and investigations that I had completely forgotten about Brenda. She had been missing from the 1963 version of Royd's Hall for weeks and there would be quite a bit of concern for her whereabouts. Numerous futile searches would have been carried out.

I finally managed to have a word with her one evening before we retired to bed.
"Do you worry about things in 1963?"
"What do you mean?"
"They'll be looking for you in 1963. Remember you've gone missing!"
"Don't care. I love it here with you and nursing. We're doing a really worthwhile job aren't we?"
"Yes, I suppose we are. But a younger version of you is going to arrive at Royd's Hall at some time, so you can't stay here for ever." I had explained all this to Brenda

before on our first visit to 1940 but clearly it needed spelling out again.

"What do you mean?"
"How old were you when you were sent to Royd's Hall by the doctors and your parents?"
She looked sullen. "I was fourteen years old. It was 1954 when I arrived here."
"You cannot be here when that happens, can you?"
"No, I suppose not but I have fourteen years in which to leave and go back to 1963."

"It won't be 1963 when you return. It will be another year depending on how long you stay and things will be different. Things change very rapidly. You won't fit in!"
"I still don't understand what you mean!"
"If you stay here for ten years until 1950, it will be 1973 when you return. That is 1963 plus the ten years you have stayed here!"
"Ah, I understand. But I could ask someone to take me anywhere and to any time."
"You mean be nomadic-like. What's the name of that Timelord that was on television when I was a teenager?"
"Dr Who."
"I don't know what he was called, that's why I was asking you!"
"No, Eva. The name of the Timelord is Dr Who. The television programme had just started with William Hartnell being Dr Who. He can travel through time in a time machine called The Tardis."

As far as I was concerned I had done what I had set out to do and that was to warn Brenda of the dangers of her special powers.

"I need to talk to Melba again, as soon as possible."
"She's not always around nowadays. I've been on the landing several times and not seen her."
"If you do, can you arrange for us to meet? I really need to talk to her about the day she died."
"Are you close to finding out who murdered her?"
"I have some ideas of what might have happened, but nothing conclusive as yet."

It was two days later, as we lay in bed, that Brenda remembered that she had seen Melba and arranged to meet her again the following day.

The people that I had not thought about, in any great detail, was my family. I had now been away for weeks but I felt that I was close to returning to them. I needed to work out what I was going to say to them on my return. Could I just tell them the truth? Would they believe me? I doubted it.

Of course, as the situation stood at the moment I needed both Brenda and Melba in order to get home. I was unsure of what Brenda would make of 2048 but she didn't need to stay there. In fact, I wasn't at all certain that Brenda could go forward in time beyond her years. That was something that I hadn't tried or experienced before.

Eva and the Winter of 63

In 1605 I met a lady who had my special powers but she hadn't gone 'into the future' either. Maybe it wasn't possible and I would be stuck in Brenda's timescale for the rest of my life.

I was getting depressed and home-sick.

I had two questions to ask Melba.
Who, apart from Jean-Pierre, had visited her on that fateful day and which visitor came first?

The answers were Fred and Fred!

But there was a third question; why did Fred come to visit her without her sister?
Melba hesitated.
"It was personal," she said abruptly.
Brenda intervened, "But it might have some bearing on how you died."
"Don't be silly, of course it didn't."
"If you don't tell Eva everything that happened that day, how do you expect her to find your murderer?" Brenda seemed unusually agitated at Melba's reticence to give me the answers to my questions.

"Fred wouldn't murder me. I didn't particularly like him but he's not a murderer."
"He's a Chemist though and you said that you were poisoned," I pointed out.
"Thought you'd decided it was the dentist that gave me mercury poisoning."

"And that nurse, Natalie."
"What do you mean?"
"Well, she told me that on the day you died you had an accident with a mercury thermometer and may have swallowed some of the mercury."
"I don't think I did. I managed to spit it all out."
"We still don't know why Fred came to visit you on his own, do we?" Brenda insisted.

"Oh, OK. He and Jane had had an argument and he came to ask me some questions."
"What questions?"
"It stemmed from the daughter, Judy having had a blood test of some sort and Fred and Jane found out that her blood type was type A."
"And so?"
"Fred and Jane are both type O."
"Does that mean Fred wasn't Judy's biological father?"
"I don't really know. It might have done. I don't know enough about blood types to be sure. The important point is that Fred was convinced that Judy wasn't his and in the course of the heated argument, Jane confessed that there was a chance that Judy wasn't his! He came to see if I knew who the real father was."

"And did you?" I asked.
"Yes, I knew. I had my suspicions from the start. The dates of Judy's birth just didn't seem to tally."
"Did you tell him who you thought the father was?
"No, of course not! It's not my style to spread rumours."
"But you knew and therefore it wouldn't be a rumour, would it?" said Brenda.

Eva and the Winter of 63

"Yes, I knew but I wasn't going to tell him. He got quite angry with me and left."

"Who is the father then?" Brenda was persistent.
"I'd rather not say."
"It's Jean-Pierre isn't it?" I took a stab in the dark.

She hesitated and then nodded.
"Did you say anything to Jean-Pierre when he came to visit you that day?"
"He was very agitated. I think he knew what had happened between Fred and Jane. He kept pleading with me not to say anything. I said I wouldn't but he kept on at me. You know how emotional the French can get. In the end I had to ask him to leave."
"Did you eat or drink anything while either Fred or Jean-Pierre were with you?"
"Not with Fred. He didn't stay for too long and I had just had a morning tea."

"With Jean-Pierre?"
"I made a coffee as I normally did when he came for a chat."
"Did you eat anything?"
"I don't think so. Oh, wait a minute! J-P brought some Belgian chocolates. I really liked them. Strawberry truffles are my favourite."
"How many did you have?"
"Just the one I think and then he took the rest away with him. Said that he was going give the rest to Judy. I don't know why, it wasn't her birthday or anything, but that was J-P, always very generous to women!"

With that Brenda and I went back to work.
"You know what happened don't you, Eva?" Brenda said as we descended the stairs.
"I think we both do."

Over the next week or so we had quite an influx of patients due to the bombings that were now taking place on the cities in Yorkshire. I really didn't know what to do. I could tell Melba our suspicions or I could confront Jean-Pierre with our allegations. Neither action filled me with joy.

As it happened, fate took control; Jean-Pierre came to visit me again. At first it was cordial enough. He asked how my investigations were going and I said I had a pretty good idea how Melba had died.

Outwardly, he managed not to react but his eyes told me that he was shocked at my revelation.
"Who was it?"
I hesitated. I didn't want a scene. I wasn't one hundred percent certain I was right, so I generalised in a pathetic attempt to conceal the fact I knew who had killed her.

"The murderer, for that was what the person was, visited Melba on the day she died. This person came bearing a gift of her favourite chocolates but the one she would choose was laced with a very strong poison that killed her within minutes. This person had heard of Melba's dental treatment and her accident with the thermometer that morning. The murderer pretended to go to the police and reported that the autopsy said she had an unusual amount of mercury in her system. This was an attempt to mislead me and it did for a time, particularly when I heard about Melba's accident with the thermometer from the nurse called Natalie."

There was a moment's silence and then Jean-Pierre asked.
"Why would this person murder such a sweet lady?"
"Because the murderer was scared that she would tell someone about a family secret."
"What family secret?"
I looked at him. He was really trying hard to wring out of me what we both knew was the truth."
"The one involving her sister Jane and who the biological father of her daughter Judy really was. Maybe her sister had contacted the murderer after she had had a violent argument with her husband about the matter. The murderer decided then that he had to do something drastic to preserve his reputation."

Tears rolled down his cheeks.
"Why did you do it? She didn't deserve to die. She wouldn't have told anyone. She loved you!"
"I really don't know. Pride? Fear? Jealousy? Anger? Any of these or maybe all of them."

We sat there for some minutes without speaking and then he asked, "What are you going to do?"
"I have no concrete evidence. There was no autopsy and Melba has been laid to rest. I had only one reason to track down the murderer and that was a selfish reason so Melba would help me return home."

"Return home?"
"It's a long, long story which is difficult to believe, so I will leave it to someone else to decide what I must do next."

"Who will that be?"
"Melba Bartle, I will ask her to decide what I should do next."
"But she's . . ."
"Dead, yes, but I have a friend who is capable of talking to the dead. A sort of medium and I will ask her to get an answer from Melba."
"Whatever happens, please don't tell Fred about Judy. It would ruin both their lives, and he has been a good father."
"I should have realized that there was more than just a friendly relationship between you and Judy. You became all emotional as you described her to me."
"She is so lovely."

As we parted, I didn't feel too sorry for him despite his tears. He had killed someone for a whole range of emotions that humans should be able to contain without the need to resort to murder.

Homeward bound?

"It was Jean-Pierre." I announced to Brenda that night as we made our preparations for much-needed sleep.

"What are you going to do?"
"I need a final few words with Melba and then I'll leave the decision to her. Then I must ask you a very big favour."
"What?"
"Please take me home!"
"Of course. You've been a real friend to me and as I have said before, you have changed my life for ever."
"I may have changed more than your life on this trip, but please, please be careful, Brenda. There are a lot of dangers that come with the special powers that you have been given. I think I'm pleased my powers are disappearing and I can now return to a normal life. I say 'return' but in fact my life has never been normal for as long as I can remember, unless talking to the dead is normal."

"But meeting you, Eva, has meant that I won't spend my whole life in an institution for the potentially insane. I think I now understand what I can do with my life and without you I would never have known."

"Goodnight. See you in the morning."

Hopefully, what was to be my last day in 1940 started with yet more bright sunshine and hard work. Brenda had arranged to meet Melba that afternoon.

I was both excited and nervous about how the day might end. There were lots of 'ifs' and 'buts' to be negotiated. The plan was simple. I tell Melba what I believed to be the truth that Jean-Pierre had murdered her and why; ask what she wanted me to do; do it and then get Brenda and her to take me home!

I found myself saying 'goodbye' to all my patients and work colleagues whom I hoped I would never see again. Some gave me funny looks. "You going somewhere?"
"Perhaps," I had replied.
"Leaving us in our hour of need?"
"Got a boyfriend?"
"Got a transfer?"

Nobody asked, "Are you going back home to the year 2048?"

What I hoped would be my penultimate meeting with Melba started just after two o'clock. Brenda and I had

Eva and the Winter of 63

to wait until the landing was clear before we started our meeting.

Melba's first response was one of disbelief, but when I told her of Jean-Pierre's confession and what had happened, she came around to the fact that what I said was more than likely accurate.

"What do you want me to do? Go to the police?"
She thought for a moment.
"I'm upset and you should never make important decisions when you're upset."
"It would be difficult to prove if Jean-Pierre did not confess to the police. Some of that mercury that you swallowed might have had some effect on you."
"Yes, I suppose you're right. Shall we let sleeping dogs lie?"
"Probably for the best. You could always get your own back by using Brenda to haunt him for the rest of his life."
"That could be fun," said Brenda.

"Yes, meeting him face to face might be the best punishment for him," agreed Melba.
"OK, with that sorted, can I go home now please?"
"Have you any idea what this place looks like in 2048?" said Brenda.
"No, I don't. You can have a look when we get there and then come back here as soon as you've dropped me off!"
"I'm really happy here so I won't stay long in 2048."

She didn't stay long in 2048 because she didn't make it into 2048!

Late that afternoon at about 4.30pm Brenda and I had walked hand in hand towards Melba's 'corridor of transit' and onto the land where Royd's Hall stood in 2048.

It was a very modern office-block!

The shell of Royd's Hall was there but not in the form that anyone would have recognised.

I turned to thank Brenda but she wasn't there. Maybe the corridor had some kind of block in it so that those with special powers could not go beyond their time on earth. I was glad I could not go to 2448 but sad that I had been robbed of the opportunity to thank Brenda one last time.

Although I couldn't see or hear Melba, I said my last thanks to her and I am sure that I received a reciprocal 'thank you'. I was all alone but back home!

The Final Curtain

I took the public electric hover-bus back home. I used my Computer Controlled Card that the 1963 police had returned to me for payment. These public forms of transport were very ECO friendly now all the oil had disappeared. I sat there looking out high over the countryside and felt much as John must have done when he took Valentine home in his car after our first trip into the past. I could almost see the sea which really showed how things had changed since 1963. With the melting of the ice-caps there was a lot more ocean around and far less land. Still there had been some benefit in this. Desalination plants throughout the world had meant that no-one went without water at any time and even the old-fashioned reservoir system for storing water had been improved with the scientists' ability to control the weather within the earth's atmosphere.

My position wasn't quite as bad as John's was at that time. I wouldn't be locked up for kidnapping two children but I still had a lot of explaining to do to my husband David and my children. They must have thought that I had run off and abandoned them.

I resolved that I must tell the truth no matter what they thought of me. The problem was that I could no longer use my powers to show them what I could see or do.

As expected, David didn't believe my story but the children were really happy that I was back after all the time that I had spent away from them.

Eventually, an uneasy truce existed in the Mills' household and things more or less went back to normal.

Of course, without my powers enabling me to return to the past, my antique business suffered as my stock dwindled. I even had to resort to buying and selling which was not so lucrative.

Over time, my mind went back to Graham and Carole. I felt that I had to do something to resolve what had eventually happened to them. I really wanted him to have lived but realized that if he did, people with the powers that I had had would have power over life and death and that would not have been right.

It was a simple matter of searching the archives of the Castleford and Pontefract Express, which had until its demise reported all local news.

My heart was racing as I travelled through the papers, starting at the beginning of 1963 for any report concerning a crash at Three Lane Ends.

The bitterly cold weather and the amount of snow that fell were reported at some length. Eventually I found what I did not want to see; a small piece on page six of the edition of Monday 14th January 1963.

Police car chase crash death

On the evening of Sunday 13th January a car driven by Graham Newton was involved in an accident after being pursued by the police.

The car hit a lamp-post at the corner of Wood View Avenue and Methley Road in the Three Lane Ends district of the town. Mr Newton was taken immediately to Hightown Hospital for emergency treatment but later died from his injuries.

His wife Carole . . . .

I couldn't read any more. I had found out what I had wanted to know and that part of my life was now at an end.

As time passed, I saw no more ghosts so I assumed that all my powers had gone. In one way I missed the excitement of time-travel but on the other side of the coin the dangers had been getting worse and my trip to the winter of 1963 had shown me just how dangerous things could become.

I had had two adventures into the dangerous 17th century when I was young and in my adult life had made many trips into the past to obtain artefacts that my customers required. Now it was time to spend more time with the ones I loved rather than the ones that were dead.

To be truthful, some of the ones I loved were dead and I would miss those most of all as they had had a great effect on my life: Rebecca, Charlotte, Jacob, Brenda, Melba, Henry Pickering, Valentine Junior and Senior, John and of course my namesake Eva, with whom all my adventures began.

If my extraordinary life had taught me anything, it was that friends are so important, both in life and death alike. And if one day when I am dead, I meet somebody possessing the special powers I had had, would I get involved in their adventures?

You bet I would!